SOME TRUTHS WERE NEVER MEANT TO BE KNOWN AND SOME SECRETS WERE NEVER MEANT TO BE SHARED.

Montana Thomas goes in search of a father he never knew and finds the reasons behind his mother's years of silence.

With his mother recently dead and not even a name to start with, Montana and his brother Dakota begin a journey to find not only their unknown father, but their culture. The Indian heritage denied to them from the moment of their births.

Will Montana be able to accept his father and the truth behind his disappearance? Will he be able to accept the truths about himself once his past is revealed? Or will he wish he'd left those secrets buried.

THE COYOTE'S SONG

The Coyote Moon Series Book Three

By

Ann Simko

Lyrical Press, Inc.

New York

Lyrical Press, Incorporated

The Coyote's Song

13 Digit ISBN: 978-1-61650-248-5

Edited by Pamela Tyner

Book design by Renee Rocco

Cover Art by Renee Rocco

Lyrical Press, Incorporated

337 Katan Avenue

Staten Island, New York 10308

http://www.lyricalpress.com

PUBLISHER'S NOTE:

This book is a work of fiction. The names, characters, places, and incidents are products of the writer's imagination or have been used fictitiously and are not to be construed as real. Any resemblance to persons, living or dead, actual events, locale or organizations is entirely coincidental.

The publisher does not have any control over and does not assume any responsibility for author or third-party Web sites or their content.

Published in the United States of America by Lyrical Press, Incorporated

First Lyrical Press, Inc electronic publication: September 2010

First Lyrical Press, Inc print publication: January 2011

DEDICATION

To Bob—who has always understood my song. I love you, hun.

ACKNOWLEDGEMENTS

I wanted to once again thank Dale Rhodes, website guru guy, editor, artist, world class grumpy old man and the best friend this storyteller could ever ask for.

FORWARD

As I researched the Lakota people for this book, I became aware and deeply saddened that this culture has become all but a footnote in this country's history. As Walter would say; We are becoming a forgotten people.

This is my small attempt to remember.

CHAPTER 1

Cal Tremont found me. I'd escaped to the desert again. The one place that soothed the ragged edges and raw nerves. A sanctuary that let me breathe and gave me the peace that so often eluded me. The only place I still felt belonged to me. Cal knew it's where I'd run to for solitude. After five years in Denver, trapped in a well-paying, but much-hated job, I needed to get away or I'd go insane, so I hiked into the desert to disappear, but Cal found me. He always found me. As the only law in the small Nevada town I grew up in, he felt an obligation to look for me when I took off as a child. An obligation to my mother I thought I'd long outgrown.

I heard him coming long before I saw him, but he'd made it this far, so I figured I owed it to him to stay put and find out why he'd tracked me through thirty miles of heat-seared canyons and dried river beds.

Leaving the shade of my tent, I waited for him on a boulder overlooking a spectacular view of the valley below.

"I'm getting too God damn old to be following your ass out here, Montana," Cal bellowed. He was panting and sweating heavily as he came to stand next to me.

"I'm a little old for you to be dragging home to my mother, don't you think, Cal?" I asked, finally looking at him. It was late afternoon, and the heat made sweat bead and trickle down my back after only minutes exposed to it.

Cal sighed and wiped his face with both hands. Taking a canteen from over his shoulder, he took a long swallow, and then poured some over his face.

"Lilly didn't send me this time, Montana. Your brother did."

That got my attention. Dakota had often taken it upon himself to come and bring me home when we were kids, but he had never elicited Cal's help before. Dakota should have been deep in the middle of his last semester of med school. I'd spoken to him on the phone a few weeks earlier about our mother but couldn't figure out what this was all about. Then it hit me.

Cal must have seen the realization on my face. He simply nodded and leaned against the boulder. "He's been trying to contact you for days."

"I didn't want to be found," I said, trying to delay what I knew came next.

"Yeah, I figured as much. Montana, your mother's dying, boy. She could already be gone. It took me longer to find you this time."

I closed my eyes, trying to shut the words out, but it didn't work. Opening them, I searched the desert for some small measure of comfort, and found none.

"Where is she?" I asked.

"Carson City. Dakota's with her. He told me there wasn't a lot of time, that was two days ago. I have a car waiting once we get back to town."

I nodded and, leaving my tent and all my belongings, followed Cal out of the desert and hoped I was in time.

My mother and I always had a tenuous relationship, in part because of her refusal to tell me anything about my father. I was three the first time I asked her about him, four when I took off to try and find him by myself. She told me that I was a spirit child, a story even then I didn't buy. My mother was a pureblood Lakota Indian, and stories were her history. They were also how she explained things she'd rather not discuss, although I learned that lesson much later in life. My mother never married, and whenever I asked about my father, stories were all I received.

Lilly Thomas wore the hardships life threw at her like armor, dented and chipped, but still functional as long as she never confronted the ugly things head-on. Deceiving herself and the ones she loved was a way of life for her. It was also a matter of self-preservation, the only way she knew how to survive. That little piece of knowledge took me most of my life to understand, and it came too late in the knowing. I tried my best where my mother was concerned, but somewhere along the way, I got caught up in looking for answers. I never once considered my mother might have been protecting me, instead of herself, as I'd always assumed.

I picked and worried the wound that was my family's secret until it opened and bled. I believed if I could find my answers, the past could be undone. I was wrong. I discovered what my mother knew all along. You can't change who you are, you can only make peace with it.

* * * *

By the time I arrived, she was nearly gone. Dakota met me outside her hospital room. His face told me what words could not. I had made it in time, but just barely. He stepped aside to let me through. I thought I knew what to expect, I knew she was sick but I couldn't have been prepared for this.

The frail, skeletal woman lying in the bed before me could not possibly be my mother, my beautiful mother, not my mother.

I held her hand and she smiled knowing, somehow, that it was me.

"Montana." Her voice was so tired, and I could feel her powerful spirit slipping away.

"I'm here, Mama."

She opened her eyes and tried to focus on me, and suddenly I saw my mother there, for just a moment.

"You've forgotten how to listen," she whispered. A tear welled and tracked slowly down her still beautiful face. "Listen to the coyotes. They need someone to hear their song." She closed her eyes, and her hand gripped mine just a little tighter.

"I promise," I said, and I meant it.

Her hand went slack, and I watched as she took her last breath. She died without ever telling me my father's name. She took that secret with her. The only clue I ever had was somewhere in the Nevada desert hidden in the song of the coyote.

CHAPTER 2

Lilly Thomas left no will. No written instructions of what to do with her worldly belongings or human remains. I always thought it ironic that she didn't trust lawyers, but encouraged me to be one. I'd offered her no arguments. I became a lawyer because it made her smile, and because she loved to brag to her friends about me. I spent the first few years of my life doing things to please my mother and the last of hers being angry. I blamed her for keeping a secret that was not hers to tell.

I sent home a healthy stipend every month to keep my mother clothed, housed and fed. I left it up to her to use the money any way she chose. She chose not to use it—any of it. When Dakota and I cleaned her house out, we found hundreds of thousands of dollars neatly stacked in piles and packed in boxes. She never used any of the money I sent her, she cashed the checks to make it look as if she did and then kept it. Knowing I would find it someday, she left me a note.

Take this and put it to good use, I have no need for it.

I saw it for what it was. My mother's small rebellion against my refusal to see her. She would not let me take care of her in life, but she couldn't stop me taking care of her in death.

I knew what she wanted, she had told me often. It took a three-hour ride into the bowels of North Dakota to find her family. A family Dakota and I had never met. I had no idea what might wait for us or how we might be received, but I owed it to my mother to find out.

It was a small tract of land owned by the Lakota tribe, not a reservation or government town, but their own community. It was difficult to find, and Dakota's and my obvious Native heritage did little to warm our welcome.

Entering a small mercantile in the center of town, I asked the man behind the counter for some direction in our cause. He was an ancient, withered thing. Time looked as if it had long been done with him, only he hadn't received the message yet. Long white hair, pulled back in a ponytail, framed a leathery face and a hooked nose that appeared far too large for the rest of his features. The only sign of life I could detect in the craggy folds were the eyes. Sharp, bright, alert eyes I knew watched us no matter how hard he tried to ignore us.

I leaned against the counter he stood behind and stared until he looked up from the paper he was reading. I noticed it wasn't written in English.

"You're not from around here," he said in way of greeting.

"Wow, you got all that from one look?" Dakota asked. "You know, I intend to recommend this place to all my friends looking for that perfect getaway. It's quaint, but the warmth is what sells it."

The old man and I both looked at Dakota. He just raised his shoulders and gave us an innocent smile. Neither one of us bought it.

The old Indian turned his attention back to me. "Who you looking for?" he asked.

"What makes you think I'm looking for anyone?"

"Only reason anyone ever comes here. The police come looking for the young ones who left and now came back to hide. The young ones come looking for the past. I don't make you as a cop, and I sure as hell don't make you as stupid enough to get caught by the police if you're running."

"I'm looking for someone named Joseph Thomas," I told the old

Indian.

"Don't know anyone here by that name." He shook his head and returned to his paper.

"Longfoot," Dakota said. "His Lakota name is Longfoot."

I had forgotten that. Mom had taken an English name when she left her home. She just opened the phone book and let her finger do the choosing for her. It always gave me bad dreams to realize my last name was given to me on a whim of fate. I had a lifetime of dealing with my mother's choice of a first name.

"You mean old Joseph?"

"Well, I doubt very much the man we're looking for is *young* Joseph," Dakota said.

I rubbed my head and gave my brother a look. Now was not the time for his warped sense of humor to kick in.

The man wrinkled his face up more than I thought possible and leaned over the counter. "Why?"

Placing the deceivingly small ceramic jar I held in my hands on top of the counter, I regarded the old man. He had been through much in his life, it showed in his eyes. I knew he'd see through the story I'd concocted on the drive here, so I decided to try a novel angle—I told him the truth.

"Because I've brought his daughter home to him," I said.

That got his attention. Looking over the container in front of him, his eyes met mine for the first time.

"And exactly who might you be?" He reached under the counter and brought out a rifle that, if possible, was more ancient than him.

Dakota took a step away from the weapon. I never took my eyes from the old warrior.

"I, we," I corrected, "are his grandsons. Lilly Thomas was our mother."

* * * *

Joseph Longfoot lived outside the actual town. The mercantile owner, who told us his name was Sam Blackcrow, offered to drive us. Considering the rusted Ford Thunderbird parked in front of the store looked like it consisted of more Bondo than actual metal, I suggested I drive and he could navigate. Sam agreed.

"Joseph don't like people much," he told us on the way. "So don't go expecting no sloppy family reunion."

"After the warm welcome we received from you, we'll try to adjust to the shock," Dakota said.

Sam looked at me, and I just raised my shoulders in a what-can-you-do gesture.

My four-wheel drive Jeep Wrangler bounced and vibrated on the rock-strewn road. *Road* was actually a very loose definition for what we were on. *A slightly worn path through the desert* might have been more appropriate. The Thunderbird probably would have dropped its transmission about five miles back. At least the Jeep had air conditioning.

Through the thick dust, I could see what looked like a house in the distance.

"Joseph likes his privacy," Sam explained. "He never comes into town. I bring him what he needs."

The "house" turned out to be a one-room clapboard shack, worn and weathered by the elements. Strips of paint clung stubbornly to the exterior, but it was impossible to say what color it might have been. A rusty water pump, the only adornment, stood just outside the front door. One lonely pinion tree offered the only shade.

"Stop here," Sam told me when we were a good hundred yards away from the house. "Joseph won't recognize the car, he's likely to come out rifle first." When I stopped the Jeep, Sam opened the door. "Wait here."

Dakota leaned forward from where he sat in the back and rested his arms across the front seat. "I don't remember Mom describing Granddad quite like this—you know, the angry recluse."

Turning around to better see him, I shook my head. "It was Mom, Dak, she saw what she wanted, the truth didn't matter. You know that."

Before Dakota had a chance to reply, Sam opened the screen door and headed back to the Jeep. He stopped and motioned us to follow him. Dakota cradled Mom's urn in his arms and walked a little behind me.

Before we touched the first step to the porch, a man came out and just stood there. He was younger than Sam, but not by much. Long, straight, black hair streaked with white cascaded down past his shoulders. His face was dusky but not tanned, it was his natural coloring. But it was his eyes that caught my interest. They were a bright, vibrant green. They demanded your attention and refused to release you once they had you. They were the exact same color as my brother's eyes.

"Joseph Longfoot?" I asked.

His eyes tracked from Dakota to me and back again, finally coming to rest on the urn Dakota was holding.

"You're Lilly's boys. She sent me pictures from time to time. I see some of her in you, but mostly you both look like him." He spit the last word out and his face twisted up in something resembling disgust with a hint of rage thrown in for color.

"I wouldn't know," I told him. "We never had the pleasure of knowing the man."

Joseph made a sound of disgust. "Pah! Nothing pleasurable about it." He motioned to the vessel Dakota held. "Is that my Lilly?" His face was still hard as stone, but I thought I detected a hint of sadness creeping into his voice.

I gave him a single nod. "She wanted to come home when it was time. She told me where to find you, that you would know what to do."

"Which one are you?" he asked.

"Montana." I motioned to my brother behind me. "This is Dakota."

Joseph looked us over. His face softened as his eyes met mine. "She brought you to me when you were no more than a few weeks old. She thought I should meet my grandson." He looked past me to the desert. "You peed on me."

I tried not to smile. "Sorry."

Joseph shrugged. "Never held it against you. You might as well come in." He turned and, without waiting for a response, headed back inside followed closely by Sam.

The inside of the little house was surprisingly clean. What little furniture he had was old and worn, but tidy. No dust, no clutter, nothing unnecessary or out of place. The only decorations I could see were a series of photographs on the wall. The subject in each of them was the same. A small, dark-eyed child smiling for the camera, a pretty little girl in pigtails holding a kitten, then an adolescent still smiling for the camera. The last photograph was the most recent, it showed a beautiful woman holding a dark-haired sleeping infant in her arms.

Joseph noticed where my attention had been drawn. "She always loved to have her picture taken," he said. "Pretty little thing, just like her mama."

My mother's past had always been a mystery to me. She never spoke of it save for one time. She told me her mother had died giving birth to her. I never saw pictures of her family, or of her as a child. We had a conversation once about what happens when you die. My mother told me she wanted to be cremated and her ashes scattered over the sacred Black Hills of the Dakotas. It was the one and only time she ever mentioned her family to me.

"My father, if he's still alive, lives in a small Lakota village just outside of North Dakota. Take me there, he'll know what to do. His name is Joseph."

It never occurred to me to look for my grandfather until after my mother died, it didn't seem important. I never thought to ask him about my father.

CHAPTER 3

My grandfather settled himself at the kitchen table, an ancient metal thing that creaked and groaned as he leaned forward and rested his weight on it.

"How did she die?" he asked, his face and his voice devoid of emotion.

I deferred the question to Dakota. He had been with our mother for the last month of her life, he deserved to tell her father how her spirit had left this world. I realized I couldn't have answered if I wanted to. How she died didn't seem important until now. All I could handle was the fact she was gone. I never asked how. I turned to Dakota and waited along with my grandfather for the answer.

"Cancer," Dakota said. "Leukemia." He closed his eyes briefly. When he opened them again, he looked at me. "She made me swear not to tell you."

"Why?" I didn't understand why my mother wouldn't want me to know she was dying.

"Because she was afraid if you asked her about Dad, she wouldn't be able to refuse you." Dakota shook his head, and I could see his eyes fill with tears.

I realized to a small degree how selfish I had been. Dakota had lost his mother too, somewhere down the line I forgot that. I swallowed down the sudden raw grief that stuck in my throat and searched for the words to tell my brother I was sorry. I couldn't find them.

Joseph saved me from my own overwhelming emotions. "How long?" he asked. "How long has she been gone?"

I forced myself to look away from Dakota. This conversation between us wasn't finished yet, but it would have to wait.

"Three days," I said.

Joseph nodded and stood. "Then we best get going. There is a lot to do, and the day is almost finished. Do you have her clothes, the ones she was wearing when she passed?"

I understood the question. The Lakota felt a part of the spirit was attached to what the person was wearing when they passed on. The garments needed to be handled with respect and burned within three days after death.

"I have them in the car."

"Well then, I suggest we get moving. We can drive most of the way. That thing have gas?" he asked, referring to the Jeep.

"It was full when we left town," I said.

"I have a couple of gallons in the shed. Best top her off."

"Just how long of a drive are we talking about?" Dakota asked.

Joseph gave him a long, unsettling look. "Why, you got other plans?"

"Well, no," Dakota admitted. "But we've been driving all day, I haven't had anything to eat since five this morning and I need to pee."

Joseph turned his attention back to me. "Is he always like this?"

I raised my brows in acceptance. "Afraid so."

Joseph shook his head. "There's an outhouse in the back," he told Dakota. "I can find something for you to eat on the way."

Dakota looked less than appeased as he mumbled to himself on the way to the back of the house.

Thirty minutes later, with Joseph sitting next to me in the front seat and Dakota and Sam in the back, we headed toward my mother's final resting place. The sacred Black Hills of North Dakota, where she had told my brother he had been conceived. A place she had told me she wanted her spirit to roam for eternity.

The journey to the Axis Munda, a mountaintop in the Black Hills which the Lakota called the sacred center of the world, took us through the Badlands. A world within a world. A place as completely alien and seemingly devoid of life as another planet. But appearances are often deceiving. That was a lesson my mother had taught me early.

The Badlands boasted a fragile beauty in the tall spiraling towers of rock called *hoo doos.* Within them existed a maze of tunnels, ravines and twisting paths that were all too easy to lose your way in. Park rangers would come across bodies every now and then. Tourists or even natives too brave or stupid to admit they were lost. Eventually they succumbed to the elements, dehydration, exposure. Nature took no pity on those who chose to ignore her subtle warnings.

As daylight dwindled, we were treated to a kaleidoscope of colors as the Badlands were transferred from neutral, sand and taupe colored rock to a living canvas, with colors twisting and bending over the jagged landscape. In a moment of perfect clarity that happens only once a day, the sun cut through the haze and illuminated the rock, turning it into a living thing. We were fortunate to witness God laying His hand in blessing on the landscape before us.

Silence seemed appropriate as we drove through the twisting maze. Joseph guided us confidently. When we reached a service road leading us up to the mountains, dusk had covered the land in a velvet blanket of blues and red. When I ran out of road I stopped the Jeep, unsure of how to proceed.

"We walk from here," Joseph said getting out.

"What is this place?" It seemed vaguely familiar, though I couldn't understand why it would. I was certain I had never been here before.

Joseph narrowed his eyes at me as I took a duffel bag from the back of the Jeep.

"Did your mother teach you nothing?" he asked, his voice filled with disgust that the answer eluded me.

When I simply stared at him waiting for an answer, Joseph sighed in acceptance that our mother had been negligent in our upbringing,

"This is the Paha Sapa, a sacred place to the Lakota." He shook his head and started walking up the almost invisible trail leading to the top of the peak.

"The young ones, they have no interest in the old ways, Joseph. You know that," Sam said, walking beside him.

"Lilly should have taught them. They are *Lakota,*" he said. "They are my grandsons."

He turned to face Dakota and me, his face sad and angry at the same time.

"Do you know who you are?" Joseph asked. When neither Dakota or I answered, he told us, "You carry the blood of a proud people within you, and you have no idea of the history, the power of your legacy!"

"She told us," I said, my voice quiet compared to Joseph's. "She told us the stories."

Joseph shook his head, unsatisfied. "No, not stories. History," he corrected. "This is holy ground. Your people shed blood here so you might have a chance to carry the bloodline you do. The white man thought they had the right to take this place from us, they even broke their own law to do so. They have no pride."

Joseph watched as the moon rose fat and orange over the plains, framing the Badlands in an almost prehistoric skyline.

"You know nothing of what was done here, of those who came before you. I will tell you what my daughter has not. I will tell you, and then you will know what it means to be Lakota. You cannot take another step on this sacred place until you have that understanding within you." With that declaration Joseph stopped where he was and sat cross-legged on the ground. Sam sat next to him. Dakota and I exchanged glances, and seeing nothing else to do we sat, completing the circle.

"My grandfather was of the tribe Hunkpapa. He has told me these things, so I know them to be true. I tell them to you now, so you too know them to be true. The Hunkpapa was led by Tatanka Iyotanka, you might know him better as Sitting Bull. He saw his first battle at only fourteen against the Crow, but this is not what he is known for. Tatanka Iyotanka led a war party of Arapaho, Cheyenne and Lakota against the soldiers at Fort Laramie. There was also Crazy Horse who all his life only wanted peace, but when the president of these Unites States told the Lakota that the Paha Sapa, the Black Hills, would be forever and ever the land of our people, it was not said with truth and Crazy Horse was not to find his peace. He was killed by one of his own at the age of thirty-seven. Stabbed in the back." Joseph shook his head. "A very bad day to die," he said paraphrasing Crazy Horse's famous words, *It is a good day to fight, a good day to die.*

I remembered my history, but to hear it told on the land where it had happened was almost mystical.

My grandfather continued his lesson. "Chief Joseph, the man who I am honored to be named after, he was of the Nez Perce and called Hin-mah-too-yah-lah-kekt in his own tongue. He tried to keep his people free, not on the reservations. It was not to be. Red Cloud of the Oglala tribe and friend to the Lakota, his daughter is your great-grandmother.

She married a white man, but a good man, one with a Lakota heart. This man was my father." He pointed to Dakota. "We share his eyes." Joseph looked out over the hills that had witnessed history, and shook his head. "Too much has happened here that can never be forgotten. You remember the names I tell you now, and you tell your children. We are becoming a forgotten people, the Lakota, Cheyenne, the Sioux nation. We fought well, but it was not to be. All we have left to us is the past."

Joseph leaned forward, and I could see the green of his eyes sparkle in the darkness.

"These are the names of The People. These are the names of the warriors whose blood runs through your veins. Cochise, Washakie of the Shoshone, Geronimo, fierce warrior of the Apache, friend to the Lakota. These and many more history does not remember."

Joseph stood and faced out over the hills. Picking a handful of dirt from the ground at his feet, he let it loose to the wind. "I honor you my brothers and the blood you have spilt here and throughout the Sioux nation. These are my grandsons, Montana and Dakota, sons of Wabokieshiek, my daughter. We have come to set her spirit free to roam with yours."

I had never heard my mother's Lakota name before, but knew enough Sioux to understand the word meant *Little Light*. I smiled at the revelation. It suited our mother perfectly.

"Come," my grandfather said, ending the history lesson. "We're almost there."

We walked for another ten minutes, the moon lighting our way and keeping us company. When we reached the peak, Joseph stopped and took the duffel bag from his shoulder and placed it on the ground.

"Think you could handle making a fire?" he asked me.

"Yeah, I think I can do that," I told him, and moved off into the surrounding trees for dead branches. Coming back to the clearing Joseph had led us to, I added my deadfall to the kindling Dakota already had smoldering. Within minutes, we had a healthy fire burning.

"I need her clothes," Joseph told us.

Dakota searched his backpack and pulled out the carefully preserved package. My mother's clothes, the hospital gown she had worn when she died, wrapped in paper. Dakota held them out to our grandfather.

He took them reverently, and then quietly began to chant. It sounded like a hum on the wind, and then built with rhythm and intensity. Joseph started a slow halting dance around the fire. He held out the ugly garment that had last touched my mother and raised it to the stars. His voice was almost hypnotic.

Sam took out a small flask and offered it to me. Caught up in watching my grandfather perform the ritual, I declined.

Sam pushed the flask into my hands. "It wasn't a request."

I looked away from Joseph and narrowed my gaze on the man beside me.

"It's part of the ceremony. Calms the spirits and allows a passageway to be bridged between this world and the next. Your mother can't rest unless you appease the spirits."

I didn't think it was the spirits that needed appeasing, but I accepted the flask from Sam and took a sip. It was a bitter liquid, thick and warm. It took everything I had not to spit it out, but I held it in my mouth, reflexes refusing to let me swallow.

Sam smiled at my reaction to the taste and slapped me on the back. "Didn't say it was going to taste good, boy."

I swallowed instinctively to keep from choking. The viscous brew burned a track down my throat, and my eyes watered. I realized a little too late that what I had just ingested was not a healthy swig of Jim

Beam.

"What was that?" I asked after I stopped coughing.

"Quiet," Sam told me. "You're disturbing the spirits."

Dakota and I exchanged glances. He silently asked me if I was all right. I didn't know what to tell him. My head felt fuzzy, but I nodded to him that I was, not entirely certain it was the truth. Whatever Sam had given me worked fast.

My vision blurred, and I stood, staggering toward the fire. I felt a tug on the back of my shirt that kept me from plunging headfirst into the flames. I heard Dakota's voice from farther away than it should have been.

"What the hell did you give him?"

"He is the oldest," I heard Sam say. "It is his right to see his mother to the other side."

If Dakota made a comment, I didn't hear it. All I heard was Joseph chanting, and all I saw was the fire burning. The logical part of me still functioning realized that Sam had given me a hallucinogenic, but the larger part completely under the influence of the drug had no choice but to go where it took me. Drowning me in a sea of color and light, nothing else mattered. I stared into the flames and watched them dance before me. Influenced by the recent stories of my past, I saw warriors dressed in flame dance in the fire. Their tomahawks were red with blood. But then they became my grandfather, an old Indian in Levis and flannel, but with the heart of a people that were to roam these hills forever and ever.

Joseph danced around the fire as the flames consumed my mother's clothes. The fire flared as the thin material shriveled and burned. I was dizzy and hot, I felt as if I was the one on fire. The flames held my complete attention. The chanting grew louder, and the fire took me. Joseph opened the urn containing my mother's remains and tipped it on its side, letting the wind scatter Lilly Thomas, Wabokieshiek, the Little Light, throughout her beloved Black Hills.

I closed my eyes and felt my mother's touch, cool and comforting against my sweaty face. Tears streamed down my cheeks with the realization that she was gone, and I had wasted years I could never get back over stupid pride.

"I'm sorry, Mama," I cried into the fire's heat, unashamed of the emotions I usually kept so closely in check.

Opening my eyes, I watched as the flames swirled and danced. They were alive, and in their center I saw my mother. Sheathed in flames, she didn't burn. Her beautiful hair floated around her. She looked young and healthy, the perfect vision of Lakota beauty. She didn't speak to me in words, but I understood her just the same. She forgave me and she asked for forgiveness in return, for not being able to give me what I needed in life.

Let it go.

I heard the words in my head and immediately rejected them. Even in death I couldn't grant her that one thing. I saw tears in my fire-mother's eyes, and then the flames took her from me. It felt like a dream, colors and shapes blending and merging. Joseph's chanting, the heat of the fire, the heat that seemed to come from the very center of my being. I heard many voices, I felt the scorching fire, I saw old warriors dressed in war paint, I saw blood, my own and Dakota's in the flames.

The last thing I remember is reaching out to hold on to the image of my mother to keep her from leaving and finding Dakota instead. I fell into my brother's arms and collapsed, the heat finally taking me. I thought it might take Dakota as well. I tried to tell him, but couldn't remember how to speak. I forgot how to stand. The world tunneled to a small pinprick of firelight, and I stopped fighting. My mind blanked out, and the world crashed down on me. Darkness wrapped around me until there was nothing left. I gratefully slid into the void and disappeared.

CHAPTER 4

I opened my eyes and wished I hadn't. Pain, fierce and unrelenting, slammed into my head. Simply taking a breath made my skull feel as if it were going to split into pieces. An involuntary groan escaped my parched lips, and I realized I was thirsty but too miserable to do anything about it. I tried to escape back into sleep, but that too was denied from me.

"Here." Despite the gentleness of his touch and quiet voice, I grimaced as Dakota put a hand under my head and held something to my lips.

Vaguely remembering the consequences of the last thing I drank without first knowing what it was, I pushed the hand away.

"Drink it," my brother ordered. "It's water, you're dehydrated."

I took the bottle from him and drained it in several long gulps. It helped, but only a little. The headache backed down enough for me to focus.

"Where am I?" I asked, sitting up. My headache escalated and my stomach turned rebellious, but I tried to ignore it. Putting a hand to my aching head, I pushed sweat-stiffened hair from my face and managed to bring Dakota into focus.

"Joseph's place," he said. "How are you feeling?"

"How do I look?"

"Like three-day-old shit." He laughed.

"That good? What the hell did that son-of-a-bitch give me?"

"Peyote, a hallucinogenic. They make it from ground-up cactus, it's part of the Lakota burial ritual. Apparently he gave you a concentrated dosage. I thought it killed you."

"Right now I wish it had." My stomach rolled, and I knew I didn't have much time. "Bathroom?" I put one hand over my mouth and the other over my cramping midsection.

Dakota shook his head. "Outhouse," he reminded me and pointed outside.

Lurching to my feet, I stumbled to the door, my balance precarious. Pushing the door open, I made it between Sam and Joseph, who were sitting and smoking on the porch. I tripped and fell down the two porch steps. Ignoring the battering my body was taking, I pushed to my knees before letting it spew. A vile green *something* gushed out of me, wave after wave until I was certain there couldn't possibly be anything left inside.

Hollowed out and empty, I collapsed in the desert dirt next to the steaming pile of filth. Rolling over to my back, I put an arm across my eyes to shield them from the glare of the hateful sun. Something created a shadow over my face, and I opened one cautious eye. Sam and Joseph loomed over me.

"I told that boy not to give you any water," Sam said.

Joseph just shook his head in apparent disgust. "Best get him back inside before the buzzards pick him off for lunch."

They each grabbed me under an arm and pulled me to my feet. They were either stronger than they looked, or nothing of any consequence was left of me. I felt like a dried-up corn husk. One stiff breeze and I would be at the mercy of wherever fate wanted to take me.

Dakota met them at the door, and I heard Sam berate him. "I told you no water!"

They put me on the lumpy couch and I lay as they left me, eyes closed and miserable. A short while later I felt a nudge and cracked an eye open to find Joseph standing over me.

"Here," he said. He reached between his cheek and gum, pulled out something he had been chewing on and handed it to me. It was black, and if I'd had anything left in my stomach I would have lost it then.

"You've got to be kidding," I said and tried to roll over. Joseph took my arm and pulled me back toward him.

"It will help, the head and the stomach, it will help."

"What is it?" The fact that I even considered putting whatever it was in his hand, in my mouth, told me just how bad off I was.

"No way, no more drugs." Dakota stepped protectively in front of me.

"It's chicory," Joseph told Dakota. "You put it under the tongue and swallow the juices. It's a little bitter at first, would probably make you hurl again, it's easier to take this way."

Dakota eyed the disgusting, slimy lump critically.

"It's okay, Dak. I'll try anything at this point. I can't be any worse off than I am." I held my hand out to take the stuff from Joseph, but Dakota refused to move.

"What if it kills you?"

I think he was kidding.

"Then I would be supremely grateful." I took the chewed lump of chicory and put it in my mouth.

"Just put it under your tongue and swallow the juices, don't chew it," Joseph instructed.

Once I got over the fact that I had just put something chewed by another person in my mouth, it wasn't all that bad. Tasted a bit like really strong licorice.

I closed my eyes and gave myself over to sleep, hoping to hell I felt better the next time I opened them.

* * * *

Fate was in a forgiving mood. I had no idea how much time had passed since I was last awake, and thankfully my memory was more than a little hazy. But my head was clear and I felt rested, refreshed even. Sitting up and swinging my legs off the side of the couch, I was greeted by the sweet smell of the desert at night. A slight breeze drifted in through the open windows. Outside had to smell better than the odor permeating off my body, so I walked out to the porch and was surprised to find Joseph sitting there. The faint red glow of a pipe, held in the crook of his hand, was all that lit the darkness. An ancient bentwood rocker creaked and groaned as he slowly pushed it back and forth.

I walked past him to sit on the bowed steps and inhaled the scent of the desert. The smell of sage and yucca soothed me like no other thing on Earth.

"Feeling better?" Joseph asked me.

I nodded without turning to look at him. "How long have I been out?"

"Not long, just since this morning,"

"Feels longer," I told him.

"Always does. What did the spirits show you?"

I did look at him then. His face was red in the glow of the pipe ash. "Spirits?" I asked.

Joseph focused somewhere out into the desert night. "The peyote allows the living to see the spirit world for a short time, I was wondering what they might have shown you."

"It's a hallucinogenic, Joseph. What I saw was a hallucination, nothing more."

"Some say that is the way of it," he said, and took a long drag on the pipe, causing the bowl to glow brightly. He let the silence hang between us as I thought about exactly what I *had* seen.

"I saw my mother," I said, peering into the night. I heard a coyote yip somewhere out there. "I saw my mother in the fire," I said, allowing the memory to surface. A second coyote answered the first. "She told me to let it go."

"What do you suppose she meant by that?"

A chorus of coyotes began to sing, gathering for the evening hunt. Their voices carried to me on the wind so it was difficult to tell in which direction they came from. They seemed to have surrounded us.

"She wanted what she always wanted," I told the old man.

"And what would that be?"

"To forget I have a father."

Joseph was silent. For a long while the only sounds were the coyotes in the distance and the creaking of the rocker. Just when I convinced myself he had no comment on the subject, he spoke into the dark.

"I've been alive longer than I wanted or needed to be. I have outlived my wife and both my children. The only family I have left are two grandsons who want nothing to do me. I have seen my people reduced from a once proud nation of warriors to a handful of drunken misfits living off the white man's welfare and forgetting who they used to be."

I started to interrupt, but my grandfather raised a hand halting anything I might have said.

"I am not a wise man, Montana, just old, but I have managed to learn one or two things in the time I have had here." Joseph paused a moment to take another drag on his pipe and put his feet up on the railing, precariously tipping the rocker back. "One of those things is that some questions are better off not being asked and some answers are better never being known."

"Sounds like avoidance to me," I said.

"Maybe," he conceded. "But answer me this, what would you do with the answers once you have them? What difference will they make to you?"

"He's my father," I said, trying to explain the need to know to myself as much as to Joseph. "For good or bad, he is a part of me. I feel like I am only half of what I was meant to be without knowing the answers to the question of who he is. He is *my* history. Can you understand that?"

Joseph smoked his pipe and I assumed thought about that. I was learning there was nothing quick about the man.

"Yes, I suppose I can. Can you live with what you might find?" he asked me. "Even if it's not what you expected, even if the truth of the answers you seek might change who you think you are?"

"I need to know, Grandfather," I said, addressing the man as kin for the first time. "Regardless of what I might learn, I need to know."

The quiet of the night settled around us once more. I thought the conversation had gone as far as it could go and was comfortable listening to the voices of the desert. I heard the rocker creak and groan as Joseph tapped out his pipe and stood. The screen door objected loudly as it was pulled open, but before it slammed closed, Joseph spoke one last time, his voice quiet resignation.

"Your father's name is Jacob Willowcreek. I believe he goes by Jake Willows these days, if he is still alive."

I think I stopped breathing as I committed the name to memory. *Jake Willows, my father's name is Jake Willows.*

"Montana, he is not an honorable man. He has forgotten who he is. Consider that before you do anything with the information, you hear?"

I couldn't reply, and don't think Joseph was waiting for one. The screen door slammed shut behind him.

The night seemed quiet suddenly, even the coyotes had stopped their singing. All I could think of was the name my grandfather had given me. A name I had searched a lifetime for.

Jake Willows.

The ghost that had haunted me all of my life had a name. Now all I needed to do was give him a face.

CHAPTER 5

Sleep did not visit that night. I walked out into the desert to listen to the night, but all I could hear was the name Joseph had given me. The name my mother refused to part with. Not for the first time, I asked myself why? What was so evil about my father that she had to keep it a secret? She must have loved him, she bore him two sons. The question I always came back to was what was so horrible he had to leave? What would make a man leave his family and never look back?

My mother's stories suggested he was dead, even Joseph admitted he didn't know if the man was still alive. But I had a name. Despite a gnawing in the pit of my stomach, that I wasn't entirely sure was leftover peyote, I knew I couldn't do as my mother wanted. I couldn't just let it go.

I watched as darkness grudgingly gave way to the light. Soft shades of violet and rose touched the tops of the distant hills, breathing new life and starting the day. Dakota found me sitting on the porch and greeted me with a steaming cup of strong coffee. Wrapped in a blanket, wearing only a faded pair of jeans, he handed me the mug.

For the first time I thought of how my bother would react to what I needed to tell him. I also realized that Dakota shouldn't be here. He had a life, a future, and being here with me now, I knew he had put both on hold. Dakota was the one constant in my life, without ever asking it of him, he always seemed to be there when I needed him most.

"Damn, it's freezing out here." He wrapped the blanket tighter around his shoulders. "Aren't you cold?"

Gripping the hot cup, I realized I was, I hadn't noticed until then. I took a cautious sip of the strong brew and nearly choked. "Hell, this could stand up and walk away on its own."

"Tell me about it," Dakota said. "It's not that bad after you get used to it. The first cup kills your taste buds, so after that it goes down smooth." Dakota smiled and sat next to me on the porch step.

The sun brightened the hills and the sky was a startling blue, but the house was still bathed in shadows. The warmth of the approaching day, still just a promise.

"You okay?" he asked me.

I watched Dakota carefully, wondering if Joseph had mentioned any of our conversation to him. Considering my brother couldn't keep a secret if someone held a gun to his head, I decided Dakota knew nothing. It was up to me to tell him or not. Jacob Willowcreek was his father as well, he deserved to know the name.

I sipped the viscous brew and observed my brother. His dark hair, cut short and respectable for school, was sleep-tousled and stuck out at odd angles. It framed an angular face that boasted of our Indian heritage, square jaw, high cheekbones, long straight nose and those eyes. Dakota shared our grandfather's incredibly bright green eyes. It looked as if he wore tinted contacts, but the color was his own. I had maybe ten pounds on my brother's two hundred and just a little over his six feet, two inches, but the resemblance usually took people by surprise when they saw us together.

"Yeah, I'm okay," I told him in answer to his question.

"You were out here all night?"

I nodded, and realized it was the middle of the week in September. "Shouldn't you be in school?" I asked him. It was his last year of med school, an eight-year odyssey he had nearly killed himself for. Being a doctor was all Dakota ever wanted, all he ever talked about since he was old enough to know what it meant.

He shrugged and looked away from me. Not a good sign. Dakota found it impossible to look anyone in the eye when he lied, he wasn't very good at it.

"Dak?" I asked. "What's up?"

"I never went back," he said still looking out into the desert and the slowly advancing sun.

"What are you talking about? What do you mean, you never went back?" I heard my voice getting louder and tried to get the agitation under control. That was one of *my* bad habits. When I get concerned over someone I care for, it comes out sounding angry.

"You haven't been around much, Montana."

"What's that supposed to mean?" I asked him, fully annoyed now.

He did turn to face me then, the anger that flared in his eyes accusing me. How had I missed that? Too caught up in my own grief to notice his.

"Mom made me swear not to tell you. She found out last December she was sick."

Suddenly it all made sense. The weight loss, the unexplained sadness in her voice when I called, I had dismissed it all, making it into nothing more than another one of my mother's quirks. So unwilling to give her any measure, so angry at her for refusing to give me a straight answer concerning my father, I never considered something might have been wrong. My mother was dying and I never saw it.

"She didn't go to the doctor after the initial diagnoses, you know she didn't trust them," Dakota continued. I nodded absently, my mind still trying to wrap around the fact that I could have been that selfish. "When Christmas break was over, she got worse. I couldn't leave her, she couldn't take care of herself. I took a leave from school in January, haven't been back since."

"You stayed with her," I said, understanding finally.

"Someone had to, it got so bad, Montana." Dakota's eyes filled, and I watched him struggle with emotions for too long held in check.

If my brother had one fault, beside his rather questionable sense of humor, it was his empathy. Dakota took everyone else's problems and made them his own. It was the trait that would make him a great doctor one day, or kill him in the process.

"She didn't want to go to the hospital, but she was in so much pain at the end, I couldn't help her." He looked to me for understanding or absolution, I wasn't sure which. "She asked for you near the end. I couldn't leave her, so I sent Cal. I didn't think you were going to make it in time."

"I almost didn't."

Dakota shook his head. Big, fat tears spilled over his lashes and tracked down his cheeks. "You cut her out of your life, never once considering it might be beyond her to give you what you wanted. You just walked away, consequences be damned!"

"I didn't mean to hurt her, Dak."

"Oh, like hell you didn't!" Dakota turned and stood in front of me, the blanket forming a puddle at his feet. "Every birthday, every holiday you boycotted was another scar cut in her soul. It was Montana's way, or you walked. It's been like that since we were kids. She couldn't give you what you wanted then, so you left to find it yourself. Did you ever find anything, Montana? All those times you took off and left us at home wondering and worrying over you? If it wasn't meant to hurt her, then what was it?"

"Dak." I didn't know what to say. He was right, every word the truth for which I had no defense.

Dakota held up a hand, stopping anything I might have to say. "No, no more. I don't want to hear it. She's dead, Montana, and you killed her as much as the cancer, but the disease was kinder. It only killed her body, you destroyed her spirit."

My voiced seized up in my chest. I had never heard Dakota that upset before. His anger showed me a portion of the hell he had been through in the last few months. I'd let him down. I wasn't there for him when he needed me, I wasn't there for either of them, and the only excuse I had didn't matter.

"I'm sorry." It was all I could think to say, it seemed pitifully inadequate.

Dakota scrubbed a hand over his face. He retrieved the blanket, hugged it around his shoulders, then sat back down deflated and emotionally spent. "I'm sorry, I didn't mean that. I had to watch her die little by little, you got to miss that particular pleasure."

"I should have been there for you, I should have been there for both of you."

"She never held it against you."

"But you did. I'm sorry, Dakota," I said again.

Holding his head in his hands, he simply nodded. "I know," came the muffled reply.

"You going back to school?" I asked.

Dakota shrugged and looked up. "I don't know."

"Man, Dak, this is your life were talking about, your dream. Don't let my stupidity take that away from you."

"You didn't, I just need some time. Can you understand that? I just need some time."

"Yeah, I can understand that. Hey, Dakota?" I knew I had no right to do this to him, but I also thought that despite everything, he had the right to know.

He stretched his long legs out in front of him and took a deep breath, pulling the emotions back inside of him. "Yeah?" He tried a smile on for size, the fit was a little off, but he looked a little bit like the old Dakota.

"Jacob Willowcreek. That's our father's name," I said, maintaining eye contact with him.

Dakota blinked once, then twice, his gaze never leaving me. I had no idea what was going on in that head of his. The silence made me a little edgy, but I let it alone.

"What do you plan to do about that?" he finally asked me.

"I need to find him, Dakota."

He watched me awhile longer, then he nodded. "Figured as much. Want some help?"

"You sure?" I narrowed my eyes at him, trying to decide if he was up to this.

"He's my father too. Besides, I might need to keep you out of trouble."

I grinned and let out a small laugh. "You might at that." I let the smile fade and made sure I had Dakota's attention. "This could turn into more than you bargained for, Dak."

"I know."

"Do you? What if you find out something about Mom that you wish you hadn't?"

"Then I guess I'll deal with it," he said.

I emptied the last of the coffee into the dirt and thought about where to go from here. "We done here?" I asked, referring to Joseph and Mom.

"Not much more to do, I guess."

"Then we need to get moving. I have calls to make. Dakota?"

He looked up at me. "Yeah?"

"This gets too ugly, you can get out anytime, understood?"

"Hey, Montana?"

"What?"

"Shut up, okay?"

"Yeah, okay," I told him. I wanted to smile, but didn't.

CHAPTER 6

Joseph and Sam helped us pack the Jeep. I had no idea where we were going or how long we might be. Joseph fitted us out for a sojourn into the desert, loading the back of the Jeep with as much water as we could carry.

Slamming the hatch closed, we stood there looking at one another. I didn't know about him, but I was at a loss for words. How do you say to goodbye to a grandfather you never actually said hello to? He never mentioned my father's name to me as we gathered our belongings and made ready to leave. The information lay heavily between us. Just as I went to shake his hand and turn to leave, Joseph decided to share the story of my father with us, at least the part he knew. I was beginning to understand this was the way of the man, he spoke only when he had something to say, the rest of the time he spent thinking. My mother always told me I took after Lee Joseph Longfoot, I now took that as one of the highest compliments I ever received.

Canting his head up toward the late morning sun with one eye squinted closed, he wiped sweat from his face with the back of one hand.

"Come inside," he told us. "Too hot to talk out here." He turned without another word and headed into the cool of the little house, Sam, as always, on his heels.

Dakota came up behind me and whispered. "I thought we were

leaving?"

I shrugged and followed my grandfather. "We were," I said over my shoulder. "Now we're talking."

It was marginally cooler inside the house, which only made me sweat more. Dakota stood by the door, looking ready to bolt at the first opportune moment. I wanted to ask him what was making him so nervous, but Joseph starting speaking.

"I look at you," he said to both Dakota and me, "and I see my daughter. The way you hold yourself, your impatience with life." This was directed to Dakota. He stopped his fidgeting, gave Joseph a scowl I knew he didn't mean, and sat down on the lumpy sofa. "My Lilly was just this way. Always wanting to stretch her wings and fly, never once considering where she might be going or what she would do when she got there. It was the *going* that enticed her, I think." Joseph paused, considering his own words. "When Jacob Willowcreek came into her life, I knew he would take her from me. He was older than she was by almost six years. He kept his hair long."

"Just like the old ones," I interrupted. A vision of me sitting in the desert listening to the coyotes with my mother invaded my brain. "She liked that." I was surprised I had said the words out loud.

Jacob inclined his head to me. "Yes," he agreed. "She was quite taken by him, and even I could understand why. He was a very beautiful man."

The compliment sounded odd coming from him. Joseph no longer looked at either of us, he was lost in the past, wondering, I guess as we all do, about the choices we did not make. The ones we chose to leave behind. About which direction our lives would have taken if we'd picked another path.

"Jacob had just been passing through on his way to Nevada, he had business there, one of the casinos, he told me. Your mother at seventeen was a sight that would have kept even a man like Jacob

Willowcreek from prescribed business. He stayed, filling her head with all the stories she had been craving her whole life. Three weeks later I woke to an empty house and a note that she had left with him."

Joseph shrugged, his face betraying nothing of what he might be feeling.

"My son had joined your army and was killed in one of your *friendly fire* incidents. A man from the government, he came here in person to tell me. Brought me a medal that should have been his. Very nice man." Joseph seemed to recall the incident and then shook his head, dismissing it once more. "I had lost my son, and then this Jacob Willowcreek took my daughter." His eyes found mine. "It wasn't right, what he did. He never asked for my permission, that's the way it is to be done. He may have looked like the old ones on the outside, but on the inside, he was without honor."

There was so much more he wanted to say, I could see it in his eyes. For one rare moment, Joseph was totally transparent, his pain and anger there for anyone to see, and then it was gone again, pulled back inside of him.

"The next time I saw my daughter was when she brought you to me. She was always a little thing, but now she was nothing but bones, and her eyes had lost their spark, as if the spirit within her had been killed. She had bruises too, on her arms, a faded one here—" Joseph touched under one eye. "She tried to cover it, but I could still see."

The words were a physical blow to me. I never considered that my father might have beaten my mother. She had never spoken of him with anything other than complete adoration, so it was difficult to comprehend.

"He hurt her?" I asked, looking for conformation. If it turned out to be the truth, I would find the man, and if he wasn't already dead, I would kill him.

"She never told me, but I knew. I told her to come back home."

Joseph shook his head. "She wouldn't, said her place was with Jacob, she loved him. I should have made her come."

"You couldn't make her do anything she didn't want to, you know that. If she thought what she was doing was right, she would have fought you to the death over it," I told him.

Joseph just watched the wind as it kicked up a dust devil outside, and said nothing. Turning his head and centering his attention back on me, Joseph apparently had nothing more to say on that particular point, and I wasn't about to push him.

"The last time I saw Lilly, you were two years old, and that one was no more than a babe." He gestured to Dakota, who had finally stopped fidgeting and settled down to listen to Joseph's story. "She brought you home to me, told me she needed some time to get her life together. She left both of you with me for a day, maybe two, and then came back to collect you. Told me that Jacob was gone. Just that—gone."

"Did he die?" I asked.

Joseph shrugged. "Don't know, she never told me, I never asked. I was grateful he was out of her life, didn't care how. She told me she had found work in a small town in Nevada, and she was moving there."

"Caliente," I said. It was where we had grown up.

"Yes, she wanted me to visit, but I never seemed to get around to it. Too late now, I suppose."

"We still live there," I reminded him.

He only nodded. "Jacob Willowcreek belonged to a Sioux tribe out of Montana, I believe. Don't know more than that."

"It's enough to start with," I told him, standing to leave. "Joseph, Grandfather," I corrected myself, "thank you." I didn't expect a reply and received none, but just before the man turned away, I thought I could see a glimmer in his eyes that hadn't been there before. It was all we would get and oddly, it was enough.

"Best get going. You let me know what you find," he requested.

"I will." I didn't know what else to say. With Joseph watching from his rocker on the front porch, we left, first to take Sam back to town, then to find a man who had disappeared from our lives before we were old enough to even remember him.

Something had happened to Jacob Willowcreek, and I was not about to stop until I found out what.

CHAPTER 7

We dropped Sam off at the mercantile and bought supplies.

"Do you know where you're going?" he asked.

"Montana, I guess," I said, referring to Joseph's information.

"Big place," Sam said, packing the dry goods we had purchased into boxes. "Have any idea where to start?"

The man sounded like he had information to share and as I knew nothing other than a name and a state, I decided to play his game. It made me feel better to pretend I had a choice. "Thought we would start near some of the reservations, see if the name sounds familiar to anyone."

Sam considered that. "Yup, that could work," he said, ringing up the total. "Might want to check out a little speck of a town called Ekalaka. Hear it's real pretty up there this time of year, that is if a person were of a mind to enjoy the scenery."

"Ekalaka?" I asked. There was a similar word in the Sioux language, *Ijkalaka*, it meant restless. It was a word that reminded me of my mother, and of myself.

Sam nodded. "Don't guess there's much to see there, but then again, that would depend on what a person would be looking for."

"Might have to make a point to get up that way one of these days," I said. "Wouldn't happen to have any maps, would you? I mean, in case I find the time to head that way."

Sam pulled a map and written directions from underneath the counter and pushed them across the scarred wooded surface to me. I opened the map and saw a route highlighted in yellow. I looked up to him.

"You're a very prepared man," I told him with a straight face.

"You never know when someone might ask for directions," he said, and put the map and directions along the inside of the last box he had packed. He picked it up off the counter and helped us out to the Jeep.

When the last box was loaded and there was nothing more to say, I held my hand out to the man. He grasped it and held onto it firmly without shaking it. His eyes met mine with an intensity that surprised me.

"I loved Lilly like a daughter," he told me. "But there are some things a daughter can't share with her father, some secrets that were never meant to be uncovered."

I narrowed my eyes at him and took back my hand as he released his grip. "Is there something you're not telling me, Sam? Something my mother might have told you, that she didn't tell Joseph? It could save me a lot of time and trouble."

Sam let out a breath and shook his head. "I know she loved him, and I know she was never the same after he disappeared. She stopped coming to see her father after that."

"Did you know my father?"

"I met him, if that's what you mean. Did I know him?" Sam thought about that for a moment and finally shook his head. "No, I didn't know him. Don't think anyone but Lilly ever really knew him. He was quiet, whatever was going on inside that head of his, he kept to himself, or shared only with her. But I can tell you this much—I am an old man, but I can still recognize love when I see it. When Jacob and Lilly were together, nothing else mattered. The way that boy looked at her... Well, it's not a look a son wants to think about when he considers his mother." Sam looked at Dakota and then at me and grinned. "When they were together, the rest of the world disappeared for them. But your father had a wild nature, I'm not sure it was a side even Lilly could have tamed. Not sure if she even wanted to. Your mama was not exactly a wallflower."

That elicited a smile out of me. "I know."

"Just be careful," Sam told us. "Joseph doesn't need to lose the only family he has left."

"I'm a very cautious man, Sam," I told him. "I never take unnecessary risks."

I turned from him, and Dakota and I got in the Jeep. Without looking back we started down the road, kicking up a trail of dust behind us.

"He knows something he's not telling us," Dakota said.

I watched Sam in the rearview mirror, as he disappeared into a cloud of red haze. "Yeah, I know," I said, returning my gaze to the road stretched out in front of me.

"If we push it, we might be able to make it to Ekalaka by the end of today, maybe tomorrow," Dakota said, unfolding the map he had taken from the box.

I cranked the Jeep's air conditioner on to high. "Then let's push it."

* * * *

Ekalaka is probably the most beautiful spot on the face of the earth you've never heard of. Boasting a population of a little over four hundred, it is also, without a doubt, one of the smallest. No big businesses, no shopping malls, one school that ranges from kindergarten to high school, a few local feed shops and restaurants, and a post office. It's a place where there are four times as many horses as people, hidden away from the rest of the world and apparently they liked it that way.

The prerequisite sign reading *Ekalaka welcomes you* greeted us as we drove into the town a little after nine that evening. We had made good time, guess the tourist season had come to a halt. The roads were clear, the cops must have reached their quotas for the month.

I was surprised to find an open diner on the outskirts of town. It was perfect, not only for a late night meal, but for feeling out the locals as well.

I pulled into the nearly deserted parking lot, and Dakota stirred for the first time in hours. He had offered to switch off driving, but I told him to get some sleep, I would drive. The truth was, I was too keyed up and needed the time to think and unwind.

"We stopping?" he asked, sitting up and working out the kinks from being slumped against the doorframe. "I thought we were going to drive straight through?"

"We're here," I told him, pulling the Jeep next to an ancient Impala with a bad case of rust-rot.

"Wow." Dakota rubbed sleep out of his eyes and looked at the small diner in front of us, and then down at his wrinkled shirt. "Hope they don't have a dress code."

I didn't bother with a reply and knew he didn't expect one. It was a game of sorts between us. I always thought Dakota used humor as a shield against the things that threatened him in life, as much as I used silence. It had been that way since we were kids. Together we complemented one another in a weird sort of balancing act that only we understood. I felt the nervousness Dakota tried to hide in the smart-ass comment, and I also knew that he expected me to react exactly as I did, with disdain and complete stoicism. Without waiting for him, I got out of the car and headed for the door with Dakota close behind.

There were two patrons seated at the counter. A waitress glanced up as we entered, then went back to reading the textbook in front of her, *Applied Psychology.* Another one only doing time until she could find a way out of the void. I could see it in her eyes, the bored expression that met us with a touch of annoyance.

"We close in thirty minutes," she said, pushing hair behind her ears.

Dakota grabbed the menu in a rack near the door and perused the dinner selections. "Good, I'm starving."

The girl closed her book, put one hand on her hip and gave Dakota a dangerous look. "Grill's closed," she said with an unamused lilt to her voice.

Dakota looked up from the menu with genuine disappointment on his face. "Really? Damn." He searched the counter and the food beneath the glass display cases behind it for something to appease his appetite. "How about sandwiches?" he asked hopefully.

The waitress rolled her eyes and shook her head. "We close in thirty minutes!" she said again, just in case we had missed it the first time.

"Doesn't take me that long to eat a sandwich," Dakota informed her.

Finally admitting defeat, she pointed to a booth, grabbed her order pad and came over to where we sat. "Chicken salad or tuna?" she asked, obviously not happy we had interrupted her study time.

The two regulars at the counter made no attempt to hide the fact they were watching us. They turned around in their seats to get a better look at us. They were both Native Americans, maybe seventy, or a hundred, it was hard to tell. You look that old, it doesn't really matter anymore. The waitress looked like she had some Native in her too, but her blue eyes gave witness to her Anglo side.

Dakota, oblivious to everything save filling his stomach, smiled at the girl and waggled his eyebrows at her. "One of each," he said, then as she turned to leave, he added, "Oh, and a coffee—black."

"It's three hours old," she told him, "and I'm not making another pot."

"Yeah, because you close in thirty minutes, right?" Dakota tried to charm her into a better mood. Didn't seem to be working for him.

She glanced at her watch. "Actually twenty-seven minutes now."

Finally taking note that I had yet to order or in any way acknowledge her, she turned an irritated gaze in my direction. "You want anything?" She sighed, completely resigned that she was not getting out on time.

"Just coffee," I told her.

Slapping her order pad closed, she shook her head. "Fine," she said and walked away in a snit to fill our order.

"You do have a way with the women," I said to my brother as we watched our waitress pull two sandwiches of questionable freshness from the display case.

"It's the smile," he told me, giving me his best toothy grin. "Melts them every time."

"Apparently," I said, as our waitress came back with the order. She put the food in front of Dakota and one coffee next to each of us. Before she could escape back to the sanctuary of her counter, I got her attention. I caught a brief glimpse of her name badge, and tried for the friendly approach, hopefully making up for disturbing the poor girl's evening. "Tate, is it?"

She stopped and glanced involuntarily at her name pinned to her chest. "Yeah." She eyed me with suspicion. "What?"

"My brother and I are just passing through," I lied. "We've been driving all day, and I was hoping there might be somewhere we could hole up for the night, like a motel or something. Know of anything like that nearby?"

That not only got a smile out of her but a brief laugh. "That's all anyone with any ounce of intelligence does if they stumble by this hole—pass through. Not a lot of market for motels."

"So, that would be a no," I said and tried my own version of charming the girl. It wasn't hard, she was beautiful and full of attitude, a combination that appealed to me.

I had marginally better luck than Dakota. Tate sighed, and her features relaxed a little. "Look, I'm sorry," she said. "I don't mean to be such a bitch, but you guys took me off guard, that's all. I was hoping to close up a little early to get some studying in." She hooked a thumb over her shoulder, gesturing to her textbook. "I have a huge test tomorrow."

"Sorry, he's miserable when he's hungry, and you don't have to sit in the car and listen to him whine."

"I did not whine," Dakota protested through a mouth full of chicken salad. "This is great, by the way,"

Tate gave us a genuine smile this time. "Thanks, my gram's recipe, but I made it. Okay, look…" She eyed us up, obviously trying to make a decision. "You aren't like, roving serial killers, or anything like that, are you?"

"Well, he *is* a lawyer," Dakota told her, referring to me. Taking a sip of the lukewarm coffee, he made a face and forced himself to swallow. "I'm about six months away from being a doctor, but I think I can tell you, that *this…*" he said, holding up the cup of coffee, "is hazardous to your health."

Another smile. The Thomas brothers were on a roll. "I'm sorry, it's been sitting there all day. I can make you fresh." She turned to make the coffee, and seemed to remember where she'd been going with the conversation. "Oh, yeah, if you're really looking for a place to stay, my dad runs a B and B a little outside town. Unless you want to drive the rest of the night, it's about all you're going to find, until you get to Big Sand. Interested? It's not exactly fancy, but the beds are comfortable. I usually make breakfast in the morning, but tomorrow you're stuck with Dad. I have that stupid test."

"Yeah, sounds perfect," I told her. "If it's not too much trouble."

"Naw, we're used to it. Let me give him a call though just to give him a heads-up. You want one bedroom or two?"

"As long as there are two beds, just the one room would be good."

"You got it." Tate pulled a cellphone from her apron pocket and punched in a number. As she waited for the line to pick up, she sauntered over to the door and flipped the sign so it read *closed* from the outside. Guess she didn't want to chance anymore unexpected customers.

"Hey, it's me," I heard her say, as she went back behind the counter to brew a pot of fresh coffee. The rest of her conversation was lost to the gurgles and soft hisses of the coffeemaker. She came back to the table with two freshly brewed cups of coffee and a plate full of what looked like homemade chocolate chip cookies.

"On the house," she told us, gracing us with a smile that transformed her from ordinary waitress to Indian goddess. "Just to make up for being so rude to you before."

Tate went back to her book while waiting for us to finish our coffee and cookies.

"What's the deal?" Dakota asked me, polishing off the tuna sandwich and taking a cautious sip of the coffee. On finding it brewed to perfection, he lifted the steaming mug in salute to Tate. She smiled and went back to reading.

I followed suit, sipping my coffee and taking my time to answer Dakota.

"There is no deal," I told him. "We needed a place to crash, I found us one."

"Sure. You want to play it that way, I have no problem with it, just so you're aware I know better. I know you, Montana, you're up to something."

I leaned in toward my brother with the coffee mug between my hands. "If we start asking questions out of the blue, we'll get nowhere. Come on, Dak, you grew up in Caliente. How often did someone come to town that you didn't know about it ten minutes after the fact? Small towns have very effective grapevine systems. Chances are, half the population already knows we're here, what we ate, and where we're staying tonight. If I can get in good with the girl or her father, the questions don't have to look like an inquiry. We ask questions that don't look like we're asking questions."

"Ahh, so this has nothing to do with the fact that she's hot," Dakota said.

On the inside, I laughed at his comment, no one knew me like Dakota. It was kind of nice not to be a stranger in my own life. On the outside I gave him nothing. It was comforting to know some things never changed.

"You know," I said, picking up a cookie and sampling it, "that never crossed my mind."

"Yeah." Dakota wiped his hands together, brushing off cookie crumbs. "That's what I thought."

CHAPTER 8

Turns out the rusty Impala belonged to Tate, we followed her home. It was ten in the evening, and we were the only cars on the road. The two old timers had left shortly before us, hesitant, perhaps to leave Tate alone with us. Tate reassured them she was fine and shooed them out the door.

Home surprised me by being a two-story log house with cathedral ceilings and plateglass windows facing the front. It was stunning. But it was the sign proudly displaying the name of the quaint bed-and-breakfast that got my attention. A hand carved wooden plaque at the beginning of the drive showed a herd of horses running through water, hooves slashing, manes flying as they ran for the delight of it. I read the name written above the carving.

Willow Run.

Dakota and I exchanged glances.

"It can't be that easy," Dakota said to me.

I shook my head, not wanting to believe it either. Nothing ever worked that way.

Tate lurched the Impala to a shuddering halt and waited for us to pull the Jeep alongside it. The porch light came on, Daddy watching out for his little girl. Smart Daddy.

Tate jogged up the porch steps as the front door opened. "Hey,

Pop," she said, reaching up to kiss him on the cheek. "These are the boarders I called you about." She turned to introduce us and realized she couldn't. "Man, I'm sorry, I never got your names." She flashed an embarrassed smile in our direction.

Offering my hand to the man in front of me, I spoke up before Dakota could. "I'm Sam. Sam Thomas, this is my brother Joseph." I took the first two names that popped into my head and smiled at Dakota, hoping he wouldn't give me away. Dakota was obviously on the same page.

"Joe," he corrected. "I go by Joe."

Tate's father shook Dakota's hand in turn and smiled. "David Willows," he introduced himself. "Come on in, I have your rooms all ready."

He stepped back and allowed us to walk in ahead of him. The inside was just as impressive as the outside. Decorated in Native paintings and sculptures, it was warm and inviting. The colors were all earth tones concentrating on sage and sienna. It was an environment that demanded you relax and simply enjoy being in the room.

"This is beautiful," Dakota said.

David smiled and looked at his home with pride. "I wish I could take credit for it, but my wife started the business and decorated it. After she passed away, Tate took over. Oh, and knowing my daughter, I'm sure she never mentioned business to you. It's sixty dollars a night for double occupancy, that includes breakfast in the morning. Is that acceptable?"

"Yeah, very acceptable," I said. "Considering we were planning on sleeping in my Jeep, this is great. Thank you for taking us in on such short notice."

Dave raised his shoulders in a shrug. "The place is empty, not a problem. You have luggage?"

I indicated the duffle bag over my shoulder and Dakota's. "Just these."

He gave us a nod. "Tate will show you to your room, you pretty much have your pick. I don't mean to be rude, but I've been up since five this morning, was on my way to bed before Tate called. Anything you need, Tate will get it for you."

"Thanks," I said and watched as the man walked away from us. He turned a corner and disappeared, his bedroom obviously on the first floor. It was also obvious who Tate took after. Despite her blue eyes, she resembled her father heavily, the Native features clearly coming from his side of the family tree.

She must have seen my silent comparison and offered an explanation without having been asked for it. "My mother was white," she said. "Blond and blue-eyed." She batted her lashes at me and laughed. "Only thing I inherited from her. The rest is all Dad."

Tate led us up the wide, open staircase and spoke as she walked. It offered me an enticing view of her backside as she moved up the stairs. Dakota saw where my view had wandered and nudged me with an elbow. When I turned in his direction, he rolled his eyes and shook his head at me. I knew what he was thinking and couldn't deny he was right. Tate *was* hot. Her long black hair just grazed her hips as they swayed. She was petite, maybe five-two, but not rail-skinny. The girl had some serious curves going on under those jeans and all of them in the right places.

Tate reached the landing at the top of the stairs and waited for us to join her.

"Okay, we have a room with two queens and a private bath on this side. It has a beautiful little balcony with French doors that open up onto an incredible view of the mountains." She pointed to the left. "Or a slightly bigger room with two twins, private bath, but no balcony over here." She indicated the right side of the hallway. "Your choice."

Dakota and I exchanged glances. It didn't really matter, but he knew which one I would prefer and spoke up before I had a chance.

"The one with the balcony," he said.

"Good choice," Tate agreed.

We followed her down the hallway past several rooms. She stopped at the one at the end of the hall, opened the door and flipped on the light. It was charming. Done in soft hues of blue and lilac, it immediately induced a state of relaxation just to look at it.

"There are extra blankets and pillows in the closet. The thermostat controls temperature for this room only, so make yourselves comfortable." She walked in and opened the door to the bath. Gray marble and black tile, everything spotless. "Be careful with the hot water, it comes out *hot*. Had one guest try to sue us because they burned themselves, probably the same person who sued McDonalds because they had the nerve to serve the coffee hot." She let out a small sigh, as if to say, *some people!*

"What time is breakfast?" Dakota asked, always thinking of his creature comforts.

"Anytime you want it. Dad is an early riser, if you're up before him, trust me it's not time for breakfast yet. The TV remote is on the bedside table, but feel free to use the wide screen in the living room. If you can't find anything, just give a yell, I'll most likely be up all night studying."

"Thanks, we'll be fine," Dakota said.

Tate gave us a final smile and flipped her hair behind one ear, then closed the door as she left.

Dakota dropped his duffle bag and made a flying leap, landing on the bed nearest the bathroom. "Dibs!" he yelled, ending up spread eagle on his stomach.

I ignored him and set my bag down on the other bed, then went to explore the balcony. Tate wasn't kidding when she said it had a great view of the mountains. Even in the dark their looming presence could be felt. I wanted to see the view with the sunrise.

"Hey, Sam," Dakota yelled from inside.

I sighed and went back in. Crossing my arms over my chest, I simply waited. Dakota didn't need a prompt. Lying on his back, with his arms crooked under his head and his ankles crossed, he watched as I closed the balcony doors.

"So, why the cloak and dagger?" he asked, with a smile on his face. It was obvious he thought this was all a game for his own personal amusement. You had to give the guy credit though. It wasn't as if Dakota went through life with blinders on, he just took what life threw at him and turned it around until he found an angle he could deal with. Some things took more effort than others, but he could usually pull it off with a smile and a smart-ass comment. I never worried about Dakota. The day he couldn't figure out how to laugh about life is the day I would worry.

"Think about it, Dak," I said. "David Willows, Jacob Willows, that can't be a coincidence. Sam sent us here knowing we would find something. We did."

"Ah, come on, Montana. Willows, Willowcreek, that's the Sioux equivalent of Smith in English."

"I know," I admitted. He was right, it was a very common Sioux name. "But it's all the clues put together. If this David Willows does know our father and he's hiding something, what do you think the chances are that he'll tell us? I mean Montana and Dakota are not exactly names that blend into the woodwork. If he knew Jacob, he would have known about us. It wouldn't take much to put the two together. So until we figure out who this David Willows is, you and I are officially Sam and Joe."

"Well, I always wondered what it would be like to have a normal name." He closed his eyes.

"Now you get to find out," I told him. Despite the sleep he got on the drive here, I could see Dakota was exhausted. The last few days had been hard on him. His eyes had shadows beneath them, and his face looked pale and drawn.

He didn't say anything more. I watched his breathing slow, and his muscles relax. Dakota slept, and a small twinge of guilt washed over me. Dakota shouldn't be here. I tried to tell myself I had given him the choice, he could walk away at any time. It was bullshit, I couldn't delude myself, I wanted my brother with me and here he was. Dakota was right—I was selfish.

I pulled his shoes off and covered him with a blanket from the closet. He clutched the soft material and curled his body around the comfort it offered. I dimmed the lights, left my brother to his dreams and wandered downstairs. With its usual good timing, my stomach suddenly demanded food. With nothing but bad coffee and Slim Jims for the better part of two days, I was desperate for something a little more sustaining.

The house seemed deserted even though I knew better. Soft yellow lighting showed me the way to the kitchen. I hoped Tate wasn't kidding when she told us to make ourselves at home. I was about to do just that.

I opened the fridge and searched the contents to see if there was anything worth getting up close and personal for. Several plastic containers caught my attention. On further investigation, I found leftover steak fajitas and a pitcher of what I prayed was margaritas. Sour cream and salsa joined the meal on the counter. I found plates and utensils and three minutes later, I had more than a meal, I had a feast.

"Dear Lord, I have died and this is heaven." Mexican food was a particular passion of mine, a weakness that I had no desire to overcome. I would have been satisfied with a hot dog, but this? I searched for a place to enjoy my bounty, and remembered the spacious deck outside the front door and the Adirondack chairs there. I decided the night air would be the perfect companion for a late-night meal. Sleep should have been my priority, not food, but I couldn't convince my body of that fact. Balancing the plate on top of the margarita glass, I opened the front door, hoping they didn't have a security system turned on.

I didn't hear an alarm and closed the door quietly behind me. The night was calm and greeted me like an old, understanding friend. Sleep did not always treat me with such care, so I had learned to make peace with the night long ago. When the nightmares threatened the things I held dear, like my sanity, I decided sleep was highly overrated. My tour in the army was short but memorable, in that time I earned the rank of Major in one of the most elite groups in all of the armed forces. I was an Army Ranger and wore that dubious distinction with pride, but that pride came with a price. To do the job required a certain degree of aloofness and callousness that I had learned to hone to perfection—at least on the outside. The inside, the part of me that never saw the light, was an entirely different story. It was a part I tried at all costs to keep hidden, even from myself. I was a master at the craft of deception until the nightmares encroached. I had no control when I slept, and that scared me more than anything I had lived through. A near fatal wound sent me into early retirement and my mother begged me to do something safer, something she didn't have to worry over. Something like being a lawyer.

I was tired of fighting, even if it was with my mother, and I became exactly what I hated. I was the epitome of correctness, except when the nightmares reminded me of my other side. The side that could take a life in any manner and not think twice about it. The side that ruled the dark and refused to let me sleep. I liked the dark, and the feelings it brought alive inside of me, the recklessness, the anger, the brutality. If I had let them, those things would have consumed the whole of who I was. It was a daily battle just to let in a little light to hold the darkness at bay.

The refusal to give in to the dark is how I found myself on the deck of a stranger's house at one in the morning eating dinner.

"I would have made you something if you told me you were hungry."

The voice in the dark doubled my heart rate in a moment, and my muscles tensed for attack. It was an automatic response I had no control over. A part of me knew the voice belonged to Tate, and I fought the adrenaline coursing freely through my system.

"I didn't know I was until just now," I said as my heart rate started its descent and all systems returned to baseline. "Hope you don't mind, I didn't want to disturb anyone." I turned in her direction for the first time and saw her sitting a few feet away on the long deck with her feet perched on the railing, totally unperturbed by my presence. I wish I could have said the same about me. It disturbed me that I hadn't noticed her until she spoke. Two years ago, maybe one, I would never have been caught off guard like that. I must have been even more exhausted than I thought.

"It's fine," she told me.

"Thought you were studying."

"I was, now I'm not." I could see her smile in the darkness, the flash of white teeth there and gone again in an instant. "My head is full, I just needed to chill."

"What are you studying?" I remembered the psychology book at the diner.

"I'm a psych major. This is my last semester, and it is less than fun."

"There's a college around here?" I pictured the area in my head and couldn't figure out where she would go that would be commutable.

"I wish," she said, her voice taking on a sense of longing. "Dad needed help with the B and B, I couldn't just leave him. He never really got over my mom's death. I take online courses," she explained. "Go into Billings once a week for clinical. Took forever to get my credits, but what are you going to do?"

"What happens when you do graduate?" I asked. "Doesn't seem like an area that could support a thriving psychoanalyst."

She let out a laugh, and the darkness seemed to brighten just a little. The demons threatening in the shadows retreated. "You've been here all of, what? Four hours, and you have that figured out already. You're very quick."

I couldn't help but return the smile. "So I've been told. Have you lived here long?"

"Twenty-four years, six months and twelve days—wait—" She looked at her watch. "Make that thirteen days. "You and your brother showing up at the diner is the most excitement this place has seen in a very long time."

"Exciting? Wow, I am seriously sorry about that." I gave her a quiet laugh. I was having an actual conversation and enjoying it, for me that was amazing.

"Hey, Montana Thomas, you want to tell me why you and your brother, who I highly doubt is named Joe, are lying to me and my father about who you are?"

My heart did a flip in my chest, everything went on alert, but I remained calm on the outside. "You get right to the point, don't you?" I took a sip of the margarita, trying to figure out how she knew my name.

"Don't see any reason not to. How about answering my question?"

"How'd you find out?" I was stalling for time, desperately trying to come up with a story. I kept circling back to the truth and just as quickly kept dismissing it. I was convinced the truth would get me nothing but more questions.

"I jimmied the lock on your Jeep, took your registration, still have it in case you're wondering. Unless you stole the Jeep, your name is Montana Lee Thomas, very cool name, by the way, you are twenty-nine years old and currently reside in Caliente, Nevada. According to what I found out about you in a Google search, you did a two-year stint in the army—Rangers—again, very cool, and were medically discharged after a mortar round almost killed you. Nearly severed your right leg, you almost bled out before they got you to a medi-vac. After recuperating, you attended Harvard law, an accelerated program, graduated with honors and have worked for a very prestigious law firm in Denver for the last few years."

I was impressed and a little intimidated but tried not to let her know. "Gee, care to tell me how many girls I slept with in high school?"

"With that face and that bod? I would say half the female population of Nevada. But give me a few minutes and I could probably find out."

"I have no doubt." My appetite was suddenly gone, and I put the nearly full plate on the deck floor and turned to face her. Sitting back in the Adirondack, I crossed one ankle over a knee and strove for a look of indifference. I was grateful for the distance between us, so she couldn't see the sweat beading on my face, despite the coolness of the night.

"What do you want to know?" I asked her, still trying to come up with a story that would placate her.

"How about the truth? That would be a refreshing novelty right about now."

I watched her face as she looked at me. Even in the dark I could see the blue of her eyes. She didn't look mad, simply curious, but I had a feeling that there existed a lethal force that for now lay dormant just beneath the surface.

"I met my grandfather for the first time just a little over two days ago. I brought him my mother's ashes. We set them free up in the Paha Sapa, like she wanted."

"The Black Hills," she said.

I nodded, grateful for the lack of sympathy over my mother's death, I didn't think I could have taken it just then. "I never knew my father," I told her. "Not even his name. He disappeared from our lives just after Dakota was born."

"I *knew* he wasn't a Joe!"

Ignoring the comment, I continued on. The truth wanted to be told, and I couldn't seem to stop it. For better or worse, Tate Willows had just become my confidant.

"My grandfather told me something I tried to get out of my mother all of her life—my father's name."

"And that name brought you here?" she asked.

"Yeah, it did." I paused, unsure of how she would take the next part of my story. "Tate, my grandfather told me my father's name was Jacob Willowcreek. He told me, the last he knew, he went by Jake Willows."

She seemed wholly unimpressed. "And that's supposed to do what? Awe me? Humble me? Make me go, oooo—your father and my father have the same last name?"

"The thought did cross my mind," I admitted.

"Oh, please, do you have any idea how many Willows and Willowcreeks there are in this area? You can't swing a dream catcher around here without hitting one." She took her feet off the railing and leaned her arms on her knees as she regarded me. Her hair fell forward around her face, nearly touching the ground. It transfixed me for a moment, all I wanted to do was touch it.

"So, do you mind telling me why you thought you had to lie?"

I looked at her until I couldn't take the naked scrutiny any longer and then settled my gaze on the darkness, almost welcoming the demons waiting for me there. They never demanded anything, they only took.

"I mean, I opened my home to you and you *lie* to me?"

I was heading toward contrite right up until then. Her indignation was one push too many. My anger slipped the leash just a little and met hers head on. Who did this girl think she was? She knew nothing more about me than what an internet search could show her. She'd lived her entire life in the sheltered security of this tiny community, always looking for a way out, but never living life in the process. Dakota and I were just an adventure she intended to live through vicariously. She had no idea what my life was like, what I'd been through. It was one thing to read about someone's life, quite another to live it.

"You know, I do mind," I said, standing to face her. She leaned back a little as I took a step toward her. "Give me one good reason why I should justify myself to you, just one."

A smug smile played across her lips as she made herself comfortable in the chair once more. I didn't like that smile, she was far too comfortable with it.

"Because I know every soul, living or dead, that has ever called this place home. I can help you, Montana Thomas. I just might be the only one in this little God-forsaken piece of hell who can. You want to find your father? Then you need me."

I looked at the self-satisfied smile on her face as I ran a hand through my hair. How had this ended up with her being the one in control? I really must've been off my game to have no other choice but to let her in. All in all, I was not ending the day well.

"I don't have a choice, do I?" I asked, resigned to my fate.

"No, not really."

"What about your father? Does he need to know?" I asked.

"I never lied to him before."

"Uh-huh, sure," I challenged her.

"Well, he's never caught me," she conceded, still smiling.

"Then what he doesn't know can't hurt him. I would rather keep this between us for now. The more people that know about this, the greater the chance that someone who knows something about my father might hear I'm looking for him and bolt, or worse, warn him."

"Fair enough," Tate said. "But if he asks me outright, I'll have to tell him."

"Fair enough," I agreed. "Tate, what if you find something you wish you hadn't?"

"Then I guess I can't say you didn't warn me." Standing, she flashed me the know-it-all grin once more and headed back inside. "See you in the morning, Montana Thomas, ahh wait—I mean Sam." She laughed as she closed the door, leaving me alone with a lot more than just my thoughts for company.

What the hell did I just do?

I heard the coyotes again somewhere in the hills. The demons were there, waiting just beyond the light. They sensed the weakness in me and gathered for the attack, so to keep both them and sleep waiting, I reached in my pocket for my phone. The panel lit up, and I punched in a number I knew well. I never worried about the time, Ito often battled the same nightly enemy and even if he didn't he wouldn't begrudge me the late-night call.

"Montana," my friend answered on the second ring. "I heard about your mama, I am sorry, my friend."

I couldn't go there, not even with Ito. "I need a favor."

His deep chuckle echoed through the miles. "Now there's something new. What can I do for you?"

"I need you to do an identity search for me. I don't have time to explain, but I don't have access to a computer or I would do it myself."

"Just give me a name," Ito said. And there it was, that unspoken bond, the trust that required no explanation or apology. I would do the same for him, that too was understood. It was Ito who'd saved me when that mortar shell nearly killed me. His hand that had kept the flow of blood at bay until the medi-vac made it through to us.

"Tate Willows." I spelled it for him. "I don't know if that's a nickname or proper. Twenty-four, a student, taking online psych courses." I gave Ito the name of the university in Billings in case that's where Tate did her clinical.

"And you want this now," Ito said, knowing full well the answer.

"I'll wait," I told him.

"Give me twenty," he said and disconnected the call.

I hit *end* and peered up to the star-filled sky. I stepped out to the lawn for a better view and raised my hand above my head. Spreading my fingers wide, I covered an entire galaxy of stars. I picked one and brought my finger and thumb together until I held the fate of a single star in my grasp, all I had to do was squeeze. The seven sisters were off to my left, clustered together for comfort, I liked to think. I counted six of the tightly formed constellation, knowing the seventh liked to hide—the shy sister my mother used to tell me.

She hides behind her sisters because she thinks she is homely, but her beauty far surpasses her sisters. Her sisters know this and keep her hidden for fear that she will outshine them. They keep her in the dark, shielding her from the truth.

Much like my mother had shielded me from the truth all my life. I wondered what I would find now that it was about to be revealed. She couldn't hide it from me anymore. A part of me wondered if that was a good thing.

Fifteen minutes later Ito called back. I kept my eyes on the sisters as I answered.

"Tate Willows," he said without benefit of a hello, "is the only child of David Willows and Jillian Bennett. Dad is still alive and runs a B and B in Ekalaka, Montana. Mom is deceased, died three years ago, car accident. She inherited a large sum of money from her father shortly before her death, which reverted to the husband. The death was investigated but turned out to be exactly what it appeared to be, an accident.

"Tate Willows is enrolled in the University of Phoenix, an online degree program, and she also does some clinical work in Billings a couple times a month. No wants, no warrants, couple moving violations, all paid. Nothing hinky as far as I can tell. Oh, one small thing you may find interesting, she is licensed to carry—owns a nine millimeter. Listed as personal protection."

Nothing new there, except for the part about the weapon, that was interesting. "Thanks, Ito."

"Did you find what you needed?"

"Not yet, but I'm working on it. Thanks again, man."

"Not a problem."

Placing the phone back in my pocket I turned my face skyward once more and placed the sisters back in my death grip. I waited a moment, contemplating their fate, then opened my hand, freeing them.

"Am I not merciful?" I asked the sky. I grinned at my own question and wished to hell someone would show me the same courtesy once in a while.

I reclaimed my seat on the porch, leaned back in the chair and listened as the coyotes sang, their song filling the night and giving strength to the demons who still waited. I fell asleep in the deck chair with that lonely forlorn sound echoing in my ears and dreamed of a woman with hair like the night and of a father I never knew. The demons did their job well.

CHAPTER 9

Tate was right, David was an early riser. The smell of coffee woke me from dreams best not remembered. I opened my eyes and straightened up slowly. I was still in the deck chair and the damp of the morning had set in stiffness and kinks that were going to take most of the day to work out again.

"The entire idea behind a bed-and-breakfast," David said, handing me a steaming mug of coffee, "is to actually *sleep* in the bed."

I tried not to wince as my spine popped and cracked. "I'll try to remember that next time."

"I can guarantee the beds are a lot more comfortable than that chair."

"No doubt." I took a sip of coffee and closed my eyes in ecstasy as the caffeine hit my blood. "Thanks," I said, lifting the mug to him in salute. "Best cup of coffee I've had in days."

"One of my many talents." A small smiled played on his lips, and I was suddenly reminded of Tate. David Willows took a sip of his own coffee, and we sat in comfortable silence as the sun chased the shadows from the uppermost peaks of the mountains before us.

"Lived here long?" I asked. Without looking directly at him, I assessed the man sitting beside me. Somewhere between forty and fifty, David Willow's face betrayed a lifetime spent outdoors, his natural dusky coloring deepened and leathered by the sun. His hair, cut short to appease the modern culture and promote business, didn't suit him. But his eyes were what caught my attention. They were black, deep black, like a hole within a hole. Fathomless, they were capable of hiding anything and showing nothing.

"Seems like forever," he told me, blowing on his coffee. "Met my wife here about thirty years ago, never thought of leaving. I've lived in Montana or thereabouts for most of my life, never heard of Ekalaka before I happened on it by accident."

"It's not even on a map," I said. "Joe and I missed a turn a few miles back and stopped at your daughter's diner to figure out where we went wrong."

"Usually the only way people find us." He smiled.

"Doesn't seem like a whole lot of tourists to keep a B and B open."

Dave shrugged and stretched his legs out in front of him, almost in an irritated gesture. "It's not, the bed-and-breakfast attracts enough passerbys to keep it open, but fortunately my wife inherited a large sum of money before she died."

Score one for Ito.

"Tate will never have to worry about money if I can help it."

"She seems like a girl who knows what she wants and isn't afraid to take it," I said.

Dave shook his head and spoke more to himself than to me. "You have no idea." Then apparently uncomfortable with the topic of conversation, he asked, "So, what are your plans for today? Taking off?" He sounded almost hopeful.

"Well, that was the plan, but nothing is concrete. I was kind of hoping you might be willing to put us up for a few more days."

"Why? I mean you're welcome to stay, of course, but why? There's nothing here."

"I don't know about that. This whole trip was an effort to get back in touch with our heritage, the history of this place fascinates me, and Joe is a historian of sorts. He heard Medicine Rocks State Park is nearby."

"I'll save you the trouble, it's a big rock with holes all over it. There you go, saved you a day's worth of driving." I couldn't be sure if David was serious or not, his face held no smile and his tone bordered on irritated.

I tried to lighten it up a little and grinned. "Thanks, but I think my brother will still want to see it for himself."

"Suit yourself." He stood abruptly and headed for the door. When I didn't hear the door open, I turned to look and found him staring at me. Before I could comment on the question I saw in his eyes, he stepped through the door. With his back to me, he held the door open long enough to speak. "Breakfast is in an hour if that works for you, if not I can wait."

"An hour's good. I'll go drag Joe's ass out of bed."

Without another word, he let the screen door slam shut behind him. I sat there staring at the sunrise wondering what the hell that was all about. Something wasn't feeling right all of a sudden, and I couldn't figure out exactly what. David Willows had been polite and cordial even, that was until I started getting even remotely personal, then all sorts of walls went up around him. It was overtly clear I had violated some unwritten law and stepped over several lines in the dirt and the man didn't like it.

Tate's unauthorized investigation on me gave me an idea. I had a feeling that Dakota and I had just stumbled onto something that someone had taken great pains to keep hidden.

I left the porch, stopped in the kitchen for another cup of coffee, then went to wake Dakota. I knew better than to do so without being armed. Waving the aromatic brew in front of his nose, I saw his eyes flutter open.

"You promised me I could sleep in," he said, reaching for the mug.

I pulled it back and made him sit up. "I lied. Come on, we have work to do."

"We do?" He reached for the coffee again.

"Are you up?" I asked, still keeping the cup just out of his reach.

"Yes, I'm up, damnit! Now gimme!"

I appraised him carefully and decided he was as awake as he was going to get without caffeine and handed him the mug. Sitting down on the bed next to him, I let him in on my conversation with Tate last night, and with David just a few moments ago. I kept what I had learned from Ito to myself, it wasn't anything he needed to know.

"Something is off, Dak. Don't ask me what yet, because I don't know, but I intend to find out."

"And the hot chick is going to help? I can live with that."

"The hot chick is trouble," I told him. "She's in the middle of something and doesn't even realize it."

"You've been doing the lawyer thing for too long, there isn't always a smoking gun and the closets don't have to have skeletons in them," Dakota said, putting the coffee down and heading for the shower. "You know, this could be exactly what it looks like, small-town girl looking for a way out and an overprotective father feeling abandoned. No great mystery, and the town? It's behaving exactly as it should toward the evil strangers." He mimicked a few bars of the theme from *The Twilight Zone.* "Come on, Montana, lighten up," he told me as he disappeared behind the bathroom door.

"Yeah, maybe," I said to myself. But I couldn't quite convince the nagging voice in the back of my head that everything was as it seemed. In my world nothing ever was.

* * * *

Breakfast was as good as the coffee had been. David had it ready and waiting, but didn't join us. I found him in the back of the house, splitting logs for the wood burner and fireplace. He had his sleeves rolled up, despite the cooler temperatures of the day. Fall had taken hold, chasing summer away and making the season all its own. It was clear David Willows did all his own upkeep. I would have a hard time keeping up with the rhythm and pace he set for himself. A respectable pile of split logs lay on one side of him and ones waiting their turn on the other. He saw me watching him, notched the axe into the last log he'd split and pulled the work gloves from his hands. Wiping his face with the back of one arm, he acknowledged me with a slight head bob and started in my direction.

"Get breakfast?" he asked.

"Yeah, thanks. Here." I handed him cash for last night and another sixty for tonight. "I just want to make sure you hold the room for us, not sure what time we might be back tonight."

He took the money and pushed it in his front pocket. "No problem. I'll have Tate clean your room when she gets back from Billings later today. If the door's locked when you get in, key's under the mat."

"Okay, thanks," I said and turned to leave. I felt his eyes on my back the entire way inside.

Dakota was waiting for me in the Jeep. He had rolled the top down despite the cooler temperatures. "Where to, Kimosabe?" he asked, with a smile on his face and a sweet roll nabbed from the table in his hand.

I could only sigh. "Library," I told him.

"Wow, the intellectual hotspot of town. Mind telling me why?"

"I need a computer."

"There are computers in the house, aren't there?" he asked between bites of sweet roll.

"Yes, and if you get any of that on my seats, you will find yourself detailing the inside of my Jeep. A computer is like a diary," I said. "If you want to know anything about a person, all you have to do is look in their hard drive. It has no secrets. I would rather David Willows not know what I'm researching."

"And what exactly would that be?" Dakota asked, looking for something to wipe his sticky fingers on. Reaching over, I opened the glove compartment and pulled out a pack of hand wipes. "I think you were a Jewish mother in another life," Dakota said, opening the wipes and cleaning his hands.

Ignoring the comment, I answered his question. "We are researching David Willows."

The library surprised me. I was expecting a small one-room building with a twenty-year-old Mac to contend with. Instead, with directions from a young mother pushing a double stroller along Main Street, I was pleasantly greeted with a spacious, contemporary, three-story building with a glass front and state-of-the-art technology. The sign out front was what really took me by the short and curlies and wouldn't let go.

Willowcreek Memorial Library.

"I think I'm beginning to see a theme emerge here," Dakota said.

"Curiouser and curiouser," I agreed.

"Could be a coincidence," Dakota suggested as we walked up the sidewalk to the glass doorway.

"Absolutely," I said, pulling on the brass handle.

"Damn, I hate it when you agree with me," Dakota said, following me inside.

I paused to get my bearings, and an older Native woman approached us. According to the badge pinned to her chest, her name was Nona and apparently she worked here.

"Can I help you find something?" she asked.

"I need a computer," I said.

"Research or reading?" she asked, pushing a stray silver lock that had escaped, back into the severe bun it had been forced into. Why were all librarians bun-wearing old ladies who smelled of mothballs? I had never once seen anyone under the age of fifty working in a library.

"Both," I told Nona, and flashed a smile. I have been told my smile could charm a bear from his honey. Apparently Nona hadn't been made aware of this widely known fact.

"Are you a member?" she asked, daring me to deny what she already knew.

"That would be a no," I told her, the smiling faltering a little under her scrutiny.

"Then there's a ten-dollar charge for the use of all computers, and printers cost a dime a page, but you need to come to me for the key code first. Half-hour limit, so you don't tie up the resources."

I looked around the nearly empty room. Only a few patrons in the reading room, not one soul near the computer area, even the research area was deserted.

Nona saw where I had looked and shrugged. "Those are the rules, nothing I can do about it."

Dakota gently nudged me aside and gave a little grin at the woman, holding out a twenty dollar bill. "Well, ma'am, we certainly would not want to go against any rules, but if that thirty minutes should come and go, and we aren't disturbing anyone, we sure won't tell if you don't."

Nona smiled at Dakota, and I think she even batted her lashes at him. Looking around the room for any witnesses, she leaned in and pushed the twenty down her ample bosom. "Well, I suppose it wouldn't hurt, just this once, as long as no one is waiting," she said in a loud stage whisper.

Dakota leaned in, playing to her conspiracy theory, and whispered back just as loudly, "Thanks, Nona. We do appreciate it." He winked at her and smiled again, and I swear the woman blushed.

I watched the librarian walk away and looked at my brother in awe. "How do you do that?"

"It's a gift," he said, and then sighed. "Unfortunately it only works if they're over sixty."

He walked ahead of me and grabbed one of the empty computer desks and fired up the hard drive. Cracking his knuckles theatrically, he waited until he had internet access and then turned to me.

"Okay, what next? I never did this before."

"You've lived a sheltered life," I informed him. "Get Google up first, and then enter Jacob Willowcreek."

Dakota did and Google answered our request in less than a second. Most of the responses were only for Jacob or Willowcreek individually and of little help to me. I saw the listing for the library we were in and pointed to it.

"Click on that," I told Dakota.

It was a newspaper article from about twenty years ago. *Construction begins for Ekalaka's first library.*

Scrolling down I looked for anything that might interest me, and hit pay dirt. I came back to the paragraph describing where the funds came from to create such a building in a place where the unemployment level had reached fifty percent.

The mayor was quoted as expressing his thanks to the anonymous donor who made this day possible. "We know nothing about the generous soul who donated nearly every penny to make the construction of this magnificent facility a reality. The only request was that the building be named in loving memory of Jacob Willowcreek. We are pleased to honor this request."

Dakota and I looked at one another.

"I don't get it," Dakota said. "In loving memory, that means he's dead, right?"

I nodded and paused as a thought occurred to me. "Or someone wanted everyone to believe he's dead."

"Yeah, okay, you're twilight zoning on me again, Montana. Why would someone go to all that trouble, and who would have that much money for something like this?"

"I guess that would be the next thing we need to find out. We find this anonymous donor, we find Jacob Willowcreek."

"And just how do we go about doing that?" Dakota asked.

"This is a public building," I said, thinking about it. "And being such, all donations made to it, anonymous or otherwise, are public domain."

"So what? We just ask very politely who gave them the check to build the place?"

I shrugged. "Sort of. Anonymous donors are only anonymous to the general public. Somebody had to sign that check. Somewhere there has to be a record of it. All we have to do is find it."

"Okay, so I google *donors for Willowcreek library*?"

I shook my head. "I don't think so, the records are too old. Probably haven't been copied onto the hard drive yet. My guess would be microfiche." I glanced over at Nona sorting books and smiled at Dakota. "Ready to put that charm of yours to work?"

CHAPTER 10

Nona melted liked butter on hot corn under Dakota's considerable charm. It was a thing of beauty to watch and a little disturbing. Posing as a historian planning on writing an article on libraries that were making a difference in their community, Dakota asked to see the records on the construction of the building, financial records, that sort of thing.

"Oh my." Nona's face crinkled up in thought. "I imagine those records could be found down in the archives. I'm not really supposed to let anyone down there."

"I completely understand." Dakota took both of the woman's hands in his and nodded at her wisdom. "But imagine how pleased they would be when they learn that you were instrumental in creating the huge outpouring of new donations to public resources that will be generated by this article." He let her hands go and raised his in a symbol of acceptance. "But I would not want to be the one responsible for getting you in trouble." Turning his back to Nona, Dakota faced me, gave me a wink, and started walking out of the building.

Nona gave it all of two seconds of thought. "Wait!" she whispered loudly after us. Dakota turned to face her again, a question in his green eyes. She sidled up to Dakota and looked around to make certain no one else was listening. "Oh, I don't suppose anyone would know. It's just me here most of the time. No one ever goes down to the tombs anyway."

"The tombs?" Dakota asked.

"Just a nickname." She waved off the concern in his eyes. "Mostly because it's so quiet and just a little spooky down there, but with you being an historian and all, I would imagine you're used to things like that."

"You would think," he said.

Nona gestured to a door behind a row of books off to one side. "Two floors down," she told us. "Everything is filed in the old Dewey decimal system. No one has had time to update it. All the legal documents regarding the donations used to build this place would be down there somewhere. Sorry I can't be more specific than that."

"Not a problem," Dakota told her. "I can't tell you how much we appreciate your help in this matter." Taking a piece of paper and a pen out of the backpack he had brought in with him, he asked, "Can you spell your last name for me? I want to make sure I spell it correctly in the article."

"Oh my! My name mentioned in a newspaper article? Oh my!" Nona fanned herself with her hand and spelled her name for Dakota who dutifully copied it down. He gave the librarian a wink and a smile as she showed us the door down to the tombs.

As the door closed shut behind us, I turned to my brother and gave him a look of admiration. "I am in the presence of greatness," I admitted. "And I am also in need of a shower after all the bullshit you were just throwing around."

"Like I said, it's a gift. I try to use it only for good." He flipped on the light switch and exposed a long spiral staircase descending down into darkness.

"After you, oh great one." I motioned Dakota forward and he started, a little hesitantly, down the stairs.

Walking behind him, I tried to ignore the feeling of unease that had been with me since entering the library, actually since the first moment we entered the diner. I felt my nerves jingling but attributed it to the possibility of being so close to finding out something about my father.

We found another light switch at the bottom of the stairs and turned it on. There was a slight delay, then one by one, row after row, the fluorescent lights came to life. The "tombs" seemed to occupy the entire length and width of the foundations. It reminded me of a scene in *Raiders of the Lost Ark*. The one where the ark is being boxed up by the government, and then the camera pans back and shows hundreds upon hundreds of identical boxes surrounding it.

"Where the hell do we start?" Dakota asked.

I scanned the room and found an answer for him. "With a little help from Melvil Dewey," I said, motioning to the card catalog in front of the rows.

It still took us over two hours of continuous searching to even find the right row.

"Hey, hey, hey!" Dakota yelled into the silence. The sudden noise scared the crap out of me, almost literally.

"What?" I asked, irritated by the lack of air and accumulation of dust that now seemed to cover every inch of me. I left the file I was looking out and stood over Dakota.

"Receipts, page after page of copied receipts."

I took the book and confirmed what Dakota already knew. If our anonymous donor sent a check, it would be here.

"Bingo." I looked at Dakota and smiled.

There were actually three books containing page after page of information on funding and copies of bills and receipts of payment. I was halfway through the second one when I started finding exactly what we had been looking for. Xeroxed canceled checks. Most of them for small donations of ten or twenty dollars sent by individual members of the community. There was one larger check for the sum of five hundred dollars donated by the council of Lakota tribes. I flipped the page, expecting to see more of the same, so the next entry almost didn't register with my tired mind. At first I dismissed it as just another local donation, then the amount of the check made me go back and read it again a little more carefully. I counted the zeros half a dozen times before even thinking to scan down to the signature in the bottom right hand corner.

I had just discovered our anonymous donor. All the spit dried up in my mouth, and I found it difficult to breathe. I looked at my brother, still oblivious to what I just learned, and wondered if he would realize the implications of that newfound knowledge when I told him.

The lights went out suddenly. A second later the gunfire started.

* * * *

I heard the unmistakable sound of the bolt sliding back on a semi-automatic handgun, and in the next instant, the slam of bullets hitting the wall behind us.

High and wide, I thought as I threw myself to the spot I last remembered Dakota sitting. I made contact with my brother and drug him beneath me as we rolled underneath the heavy oak table.

"What the hell!" Dakota said from beneath me.

"Shut up," I whispered in his ear, just as another spray of bullets hit the top of the table, sending wood splinters and papers showering down on top of us.

Dakota complied. As quickly as the brief one-sided firefight had started it ended, the gunman apparently making his retreat in the echoes of the last volley. I listened for what seemed like a long time and was rewarded by only the sound of our breathing.

"Can I move yet?" Dakota whispered.

I listened for another minute, and then satisfied that the attack was meant to frighten instead of kill, I rolled off Dakota. "Yeah," I said, helping him up. "You okay?"

"Am I okay?" he asked in disbelief. "No, I am not okay! Someone, for reasons I can't begin to fathom, just tried to kill us. That makes me undeniably *not* okay, not by any stretch of the imagination."

We were still standing in complete darkness. "No, they weren't," I told him. Grabbing his wrist I guided him by memory to where I thought the steps should be. "If whoever fired at us wanted to kill us, we wouldn't be having this conversation right now."

"Oh, yeah, thanks. That brings me great comfort."

Fumbling along the wall, I felt the cold metal of the stairwell and then just beyond that, that light switch.

"Lights," I warned Dakota as I hit the switch.

We both squinted against the sudden glare and blinked as our eyes adjusted. Looking around, I saw the empty casings scattered on the floor. The gunman had been standing in the exact same spot as I was now. The table we were sitting at was covered in fresh gouges, the old documents we were just looking at shredded by the bullets. The yellow, fragile pages littered the table top and the floor beneath it. Some of the documents were salvageable, but most were scorched and damaged beyond repair.

"What the hell?" Dakota asked again, confusion clear on his face.

"Someone was telling us we were getting just a little too close," I said, bending down and picking up one of the shell casings.

"Too close to what?" Dakota asked.

I shrugged, slipping the shell in my pocket. "The truth."

"Montana, most people do not get shot at looking up their family history."

"They do if that family is trying to hide something."

"Yeah, you lost me, again." Dakota wiped the palm of one hand on the back of his jeans, and then used the same hand to wipe sweat from his eyes.

I pulled out the sheet of paper from my back pocket and unfolded the crumpled page I had been looking at before it all hit the fan. I had ripped it out of the book and jammed into my pocket before tackling Dakota.

Smoothing out the wrinkles and fitting it together where it had ripped, I handed it to Dakota. He eyed me suspiciously, but he reached out to take the document.

"What's this?" he asked, paper in hand, but not looking at it yet. It was almost as if he wanted to delay finding out what was on it, as if he knew the information he was about to be made privy to would irrevocably change his life.

"What we were looking for," I told him, and watched his face carefully as his eyes scanned the words. I could tell the exact instant his brain received the data and watched as he tried to find some loophole, some way to refute the past. I knew exactly how he felt, because I was right there with him.

"No," he said still reading and re-reading. "No freaking way, Montana." He looked up from the paper, his face betraying more concern than it had when someone was shooting at us.

"Tell me how it's wrong, Dakota. Tell me, and show me one thing that refutes the fact that you are holding a copy of a check for a half a million dollars, made out to Ekalaka Public Library and signed by one Lillian Thomas. Lillian Thomas from Caliente, Nevada." Saying it out loud made it sound all the more unbelievable. "Lilly Thomas, *our mother,* was the anonymous donor to the Willowcreek Memorial Library."

"Why? And where the hell did Mom get hold of five-hundred-thousand dollars?"

"That," I said, taking the paper back from him and putting it in my wallet for safe keeping, "is exactly what someone doesn't want us to find out."

CHAPTER 11

Considering we were two floors underground, it didn't surprise me that Nona and the patrons above us heard nothing. Our gunman had counted on that fact as well. It was also clear he had not exited by going back up the rickety metal stairwell. Even if our shooter wore sneakers we would have heard him. There had to be another exit on this level, which meant that our sniper was familiar with the building, maybe he had been sitting somewhere hidden in the racks of books listening to our exchange with Nona. Watching and waiting. Thinking back to when we first entered the building, I didn't remember any metal detectors in place. Apparently Ekalaka, Montana had not reached the same level of neurotic paranoia as the rest of the country.

It would have been easy to smuggle a gun in, hidden in a jacket pocket or even a shoulder holster. People don't see what they aren't looking for, and who would've been looking for a sniper in a quiet little library? It would have been simple to wait us out, slip down into the tombs, deliver his message and then just as quietly slip back out again.

"Look around," I told Dakota. "There has to be an exit on this level."

Dakota agreed. He went to the right, while I went to the left. Built in a relative rectangle, it didn't take long to find it.

"Here!" I heard Dakota call from the other side of the room. "I found it, over here."

I saw the brightly lit red *exit* sign from two rows away. This must have been how he got out. I read the warning on the push bar: *Emergency exit only. Alarm will sound on opening.* I looked at Dakota and shrugged. "I think this qualifies as an emergency," I said, and pushed open the door. Silence greeted us along with the brilliant, almost blinding glare of the Montana afternoon. I didn't think an alarm would sound, relatively confident that it had been disabled. Maybe it had been disabled for years and no one thought it important enough to fix, or maybe it had only recently been tampered with. Either way, I was willing to bet our shooter knew he had a silent way out.

The doorway was set in a crevice with two concrete retaining walls, one on each side, and a sidewalk slowly climbing up to street level. The door would be hidden from view to anyone entering the library or walking nearby. I was sure our shooter knew this as well. When we reached the front of the building, there was nothing to be seen, no one around, everyone totally oblivious to the fact that there had been a one-sided firefight a few yards away.

"Now what?" Dakota asked. He still looked a little unsettled. I had to remind myself that Dakota had never been in the military. He was familiar with weapons, mostly because I forced him to be, but he didn't own one and detested their violent nature.

My brother the pacifist, it was almost funny considering I had lost count of how many lives I had taken in the name of war, or was it peace? Sometimes the reasons confused me. I wrapped the rationale around words like "duty" and "honor" and tried not to think of the eyes looking back at me through night vision, the muffled grunts of a life being extinguished by my actions. Sometimes I wondered why I was never the one on the other end of the scope, why I was always the one to pull the trigger.

Luck, I was told. Whether that luck was good or bad, I never could decide.

It was a question I never asked anyone and one I knew fueled the nightmares that kept my sleep at bay. Those eyes in the dark were my demons in the night. They hunted me down every time I closed my eyes, asking for justification. I never found any.

"Montana?" Dakota rattled me out of my thoughts, and I realized I hadn't answered him.

"Yeah," I said, shaking off the past and trying to concentrate on the here and now. "I think we should go on as if nothing happened."

"What?" Dakota stopped walking and stood on the sidewalk. "Someone tries to kills us, we have no idea why or who, and you just want to forget about it?"

I walked past him and heard him follow me. When we reached the Jeep, I turned to him. "I told you, whoever it was had no intention of killing us."

Dakota shook his head, not buying it. "Live rounds, fired in my general direction, constitutes someone trying to kill me, fuck intent!"

"If we leave, we will never get another chance at this. Someone doesn't want us finding out about Jake Willows or our mother's involvement with him. Doesn't that make you the least bit curious as to why? What scares someone so badly they feel they need to make us believe our lives are in danger if we keep looking?"

"Don't know, don't care. Don't like getting shot at."

"Not the highlight of my day either," I told him. "Come on. Trust me on this, I promise I won't let it go too far. I've never been this close before, Dakota. The answers are right there! I can almost touch them they are so close." I wouldn't beg him, but this was as close as I would come. I know I told him he could leave at any time, but the truth of the matter was I wanted Dakota with me, I needed him there. I just couldn't admit that to him. I was being undeniably selfish, but I couldn't let it go. I never could.

Dakota rubbed his hands over his face and turned away from me, looking back toward the library. I knew he was thinking of what had just happened there and weighing what I had asked of him with what he wanted to do. Finally, shaking his head, he came to stand next to me. The frustration of wanting to leave and wanting answers to his own questions was evident on his face.

"You're pissing me off, Montana," he said, reaching for the passenger door handle on the Jeep.

I couldn't help but offer him a small grin. I knew I had him, and walked to the driver's side. Just before I opened my door, I looked at him over the roof. "Nona's going to have your ass for that mess," I informed him. "I'm pretty sure bullet holes in the books are a big no-no."

"Nona likes me. I'll just tell her it was all your fault. Hate to break this to you, pal, but I don't think she likes you very much."

"Yeah, I don't get that," I said, as we both entered the vehicle at the same time.

For a while we both sat there staring straight ahead. Despite the declaration I had just made to Dakota, I was having a difficult time figuring out exactly what to do next. This whole thing was messing me up. I made mistakes all along the way. Mistakes I'd never made before. I forgot to watch my back, and I involved Dakota in something he wanted no part of. I was not being rational and worse than that, I knew it and I didn't care. All I could think of was the answers to my questions were right there in front of my face. I would never get a second chance at this.

"So what now?" Dakota asked.

"We go back to the B and B."

"And do what?"

"We wait. Someone is expecting us to hightail it out of here. I have

a feeling they are not going to be very happy when we ignore their less than subtle warning."

"Yeah, and see, that's exactly what worries me. What happens when they decide to stop being subtle?"

"That's when they start making mistakes," I told him. "That's when we start finding answers."

I knew he wasn't happy with the explanation, but he didn't understand one thing. Whoever shot at us in the library pushed first. No one pushes me without getting pushed back and a hell of a lot harder. It was stupid pride and ingrained Ranger attitude, but it was something I had no control over. At least that's what I tried to tell myself, I never did quite buy it though. The justification never made it through the guilt and the doubt—didn't stop me, I just chose to ignore the voices.

The Impala was sitting in front of the house when we pulled up. I parked the Jeep next to it and got out. It was quiet, no one around. The only sound I could hear was the quite ticking of the Impala's engine as the metal cooled down. Walking over, I placed my hand on the hood—still warm.

"Thought she had a test," Dakota said, coming to stand next to me.

"Yeah, me too. Billings is a couple hours drive, she shouldn't be back so soon." Stepping back, I looked up as the feeling of being watched was suddenly very strong. The curtains in a second floor window flipped closed before I could see the face that had just been there.

"Tate?" Dakota asked, looking up with me.

"That would be my guess."

"Montana, what the hell is going on? I mean, all jokes aside, I feel like we're in an episode of *The Twilight Zone* and no one told us."

"I never did get to look up David Willows before the proverbial shit hit."

"Nothing proverbial about it," Dakota said. "Trust me, I know shit when it gets thrown at me."

"David Willows is in the middle of all of this. I would bet my life on it."

"Yeah, well, I would say you almost did. Come on, Montana, why don't we just talk to the man before someone else decides to start shooting at us?"

"The direct approach, huh?" I considered that.

"It's been known to work."

"I don't like it, but yeah, you might be right. Let's see if Daddy Dearest is home, and then maybe we talk to the daughter, I have a feeling she's up to something."

We searched the house and found nothing and no one. Not even Tate. She had to be home, her car was out front, but no sign of her anywhere.

"Now what?" Dakota asked. He flopped down on the couch in the living room face-first, his voice muffled by the cushions.

I walked to the large bay window in the front of the room, trying to figure out exactly how to answer that when a sudden movement outside caught my attention.

I saw long black hair kicked up by the breeze as someone crouched down next to my Jeep. Backing away from the window, I crept over to the front door and quietly opened it. From the couch I heard Dakota ask, "What?"

I motioned for him to be quiet. He rolled off the couch and ducked so he wouldn't be seen from outside and came up behind me.

"What?" he repeated in a whisper.

"Tate's messing with the Jeep."

"Why?"

"What do you say we ask her?" I said, and walked out onto the porch with Dakota behind me.

We watched her for a while. The Jeep stood between us and her, so she couldn't see us. She was crouched down next to the driver's door and opened it just enough to put her arm through and then closed it again quietly. Standing, she looked in the window at whatever she'd just done. Apparently satisfied, she looked up and noticed us for the first time watching. She let out a little squeal and put her hand to her face as she took a couple of steps backward. I guess she didn't expect to see us there.

"Mind telling us what you're doing?" I asked her as I came down the porch steps.

"You scared me!" she said defensively. She walked around to the other side of the vehicle ignoring the question and tried to get us to follow her back inside. "Dad said you guys were spending the day at Medicine Rocks. I was surprised to see you back here so soon."

I nodded as I continued to walk toward the Jeep. "And I'm surprised to see you creeping around my Jeep like a common thief." I got to the passenger side window and cupped my hands around my eyes to cut the glare. Surprised at what I found there, I looked back over my shoulder at Tate.

"You've been a busy girl," I told her, yanking the door open. "How'd the test go?" Taking a clean tissue out of my back pocket, I reached inside and pulled out a 9mm Berretta.

Tate glanced around her. She looked like someone not used to getting caught doing something wrong. She certainly wasn't very good at it.

"Mind telling me why the hell you're planting a gun in my Jeep?"

"You?" Dakota came off the porch steps and confronted her. "It was you in the library?"

"I don't know what you're talking about," she said, flinging a curtain of dark hair behind one shoulder.

Taking the shell casing I had grabbed back in the tombs, I held it up against the weapon. "Nine millimeter shell, nine millimeter gun. Gee, what are the odds of that?"

"What the hell were you trying to kill us for?" Dakota yelled in Tate's face.

Frustration at being caught and having whatever she was trying to do fail miserably, showed in her face. She turned her fury on Dakota. "I was *not* trying to kill you! For God's sake!"

"You fired a gun at me!"

"To scare you, not to kill you!" she insisted.

"Why?" I asked her.

She let out a frustrated sigh, crossed her arms over her chest and stared at me. "Can't you just go away and not come back?"

"You planted the gun to make it look like we were the ones who shot up the library?" Dakota asked.

I nodded before Tate could answer.

"Why?" Dakota asked. "Why shoot at us in the first place?"

"If we were arrested or at least suspected of destroying public property, then we wouldn't have time to investigate. Would we, Tate?" I asked.

"I wouldn't have had to plant the gun if you'd just left like you were supposed to!"

"We don't scare that easy," I told her.

"Speak for yourself," Dakota said. It was obvious by the look on his face he still couldn't believe it was Tate who had fired at us.

"Why, Tate?" I asked her. "You better start talking, because I have a feeling you wouldn't want Daddy Dave to know what you have been up to."

Tate glared at me. She walked over to the Jeep and opened the passenger door. "Get in and drive," she ordered.

I just raised my brows at her and glanced over at Dakota. He surprised the hell out of me by taking two quick steps and grabbing the gun from my hands and pointing it at Tate.

"I swear to God, if you don't start talking and tell me what the hell is going on, I'm going to forget I hate these things, got it?"

"So, what? You're going to shoot me? I don't think so." She bent down and got in the Jeep. Apparently Tate didn't scare easily either. I was beginning to like that about her.

I put a hand on the gun Dakota was still pointing at her and made him lower it. When I touched him, I felt the small tremor and realized he was barely holding it together. He stared at her, the look on his face completely masking anything he might have been thinking.

I had seen that look once before. We were in our teens, and someone made the mistake of calling our mother a half-breed Indian slut in front of Dakota. They took the kid away in an ambulance. My peace-loving brother had nearly killed him with nothing but his hands. Cal Tremont had been the only thing standing between him and serving some serious time. The fact that the boy in question had a juvenile record a yard long helped swing the judge's decision in Dakota's favor as well. He did some community service, and they sealed his juvenile record. It was the only time I had ever seen Dakota act in anger.

I feared that he was on the brink of losing it again. The fact that Tate was female seemed to make very little difference to Dakota at the moment.

I took the gun from him and pushed out the empty clip. "It helps the intimidation factor a little if it's loaded."

Dakota looked a little deflated but no less angry.

"We'll play her game for now," I told him. "Let's see where she takes this, okay?"

"I don't like it," he told me.

"Me either, but what else do we have right now?"

Knowing I was right, but still not happy about it, he walked over to the driver's side, opened the door and flipped up the seat to sit in the back. I got in the driver's seat and turned toward Tate who, if possible, looked even angrier than Dakota.

"I suggest you start talking," I said.

"Not here, take the main road out to highway fifty, follow the signs to Medicine Rocks State Park. At least you won't have to lie to my father when he asked if you made it there."

I glanced back at Dakota, asking for his opinion.

"Just drive," he told me.

Without another word, I put the gun on the seat between us and did just that.

* * * *

Tate didn't need to give directions. Medicine Rocks State Park was a popular tourist attraction and the route was well marked. I had no idea what the point of the little road trip was, but I tried to be patient and find out. Wasn't easy. Tate kept her thoughts to herself during the drive, looking out the window the entire time.

The park was only about fourteen miles north of town. Another place I had always wanted to visit but could never seem to find the time. Funny how life worked out sometimes. If Tate was looking for safety in numbers she was out of luck. The park was deserted. Ours was the only vehicle to be seen in the guest parking lot. As soon as I stopped the Jeep, Tate opened the door and just started walking without as much as a backward glance.

"I guess we're supposed to follow her," I said, watching her put a good deal of distance between us.

Dakota got out of the Jeep and slammed the door. "Hey!" he yelled after her retreating back. When that failed to elicit a response from her, he took off at a run after her. It didn't take him long to catch up with her. Dakota was a long distance runner, his way of relieving stress. Combine that power with a little adrenaline and he was on Tate quicker than I realized. I could tell by the way he moved that he planned on doing the girl some harm. Dakota was a difficult man to get angry, but when he did, he had a hard time letting go of it. I don't think Tate counted on that.

Hampered by the Jeep between us, I was behind him by a couple of feet when he got his hands on her.

She either hadn't heard his approach or thought nothing of it. Dakota grabbed her by one arm and spun her around to face him. She cried out in pain as his hand gripped her wrist. The sudden turn had her losing her balance, and he let her go to fall ungracefully on her backside.

I hadn't noticed that Dakota had taken the gun with him until just now. I saw it wasn't the Berretta but my fully loaded Glock that had been in the console. The fact that he stood over Tate, who was lying helplessly on the ground, with the gun aimed directly at her, made me realize how completely unhinged the shooting in the library had left him.

I approached him slowly. Tate looked up at me, the attitude and cockiness completely vanished, replaced by genuine fear for the first time.

"No way," Dakota told her. He pulled the slide back on the weapon, putting a live round in the chamber. "See, it doesn't work that way. You don't get to try and kill me and then just walk away. Enough of the mystery. You start talking, or I start shooting, and I'll warn you, he's the marksman, not me," he said, meaning me.

"Dakota," I said coming up behind him. "She can't hurt you, she's unarmed."

"That fact didn't seem to bother her any when she was firing at us, did it?"

"Oh, for God's sake!" Tate started to get up, and Dakota fired a round into the sand next to her feet. Tate froze.

I raised my brows in appreciation. Either he had been practicing or the closeness of the shot was purely by accident. I knew I could stop Dakota if things started to look like they were getting out of control, but for now, I let him play it his way. I didn't think he had it in him to really hurt her. Scare her? Sure, she deserved that much anyway.

"Look." Tate took a deep breath and let it out slowly. "I never meant to hurt you. I just wanted to scare you. Hell! Even if you had been standing in plain sight, those shots would never even have come close."

"Why?" Dakota asked, his aim never wavering.

"Put the gun down, and I'll tell you."

"Dak, where's she gonna go?" I asked him, motioning to the miles of nothing all around us.

Apparently realizing I was right, he lowered the gun, but held it against his thigh. "He has the keys, I have the gun," he reminded her. "You give me any attitude, I'll either shoot you or just leave you here. I haven't decided which appeals to me more yet."

Tate rolled her eyes. She got her feet and wiped the dirt from her pants and then her hands. "Man, I thought you would be the one to freak, not him," she said to me.

"See what you get for making assumptions about people you barely know?" I asked her.

"Talk," Dakota reminded her. I had rarely seen him like this, impatient and edgy. I had *never* seen him treat a woman like he just treated Tate.

"You see this place?" Tate asked us. "Medicine Rocks is holy ground for the Sioux. I used to ride my bike out here when I was just a kid. There are tunnels and caves that are so hidden I doubt anyone knows about them. I found one when I was ten, as far as I know, only one other person in the world knows of its existence."

"What the hell does this have to do with you shooting at us in the basement of a library?" Dakota asked, his face screwed up in confusion.

"Is he always this impatient?" Tate asked me.

"Only when he feels threatened," I told her. "If I were you I would get to the point."

Tate rolled her eyes. "Follow me."

Dakota pulled the trigger and put another round in the dirt just in front of her.

She jumped a little, testament to her nerves despite the brave face she put on. "Would you *stop* that!" she yelled at Dakota.

"Babe, I'm not following you anywhere until you start telling me what this whole thing is all about. I'm not a big mystery fan and my usually calm demeanor has seen better days. I'm pissed, I'm armed and I'm out of patience." The finger resting on the trigger shook just a little, and I decided Dakota had played this as far as I would let him.

I put my hand over the sleek silver barrel and pushed the gun down and away from Tate. Dakota let me. I knew he didn't have to, and I knew what it meant that he let me take the gun from him.

"Well, it's about time!" Tate declared, breathing a sigh of relief and relaxing visibly as I took the weapon. "No offense, but your brother's a little whacked," she said to me.

I pulled the clip and checked the rounds, then pushed it back in making sure a live one was sitting in the chamber.

"Actually," I said, aiming the gun just past her shoulder to a boulder about a hundred yards behind her, "between the two of us, Dakota is the voice of reason."

I fired in rapid succession, hitting the rock and creating a perfect semicircle above Tate's head on the boulder. She ducked involuntarily, and then looked behind her as the dust cleared.

"But he was right, I am the better shot. I have one round left," I told her as she turned back to me. "Don't make me use it—I won't miss."

Tate held up both hands in acceptance. "Okay, I was wrong, you're both whacked." She closed her eyes for a moment, and when she opened them again she seemed more in control. "Please," she said quietly. "It will make more sense if you come with me. I promise it will all make sense." She looked from me to Dakota, waiting for an answer.

Dakota looked away from Tate for the first time and gave me a sideways glance.

"Up to you, Cochise," I said.

He thought about it, and then turned his attention back to her. "Walk," he told her.

Tate turned her back and did exactly as Dakota had instructed. I followed behind them wondering exactly where she was taking us and what we would learn when we got there. I had started this journey a lifetime ago, seeking the truth of who I was and where I came from. The pure and simple truth. I realized in a moment of perfect clarity that the truth is rarely pure and it is never simple.

CHAPTER 12

Medicine Rocks is in the near perfect middle of nowhere. Nearly sixty-one million years old, it has served as a place for vision quests and religious ceremonies for generations of Native Americans, among them the Sioux of which the Lakota were a member.

Huge sandstone monoliths stood almost fifty feet above the desert floor in some places. The Sioux had their own name for the place: *Inya-oka-la-ka* or "Rock with holes in it". The name was appropriate. The huge rocks looked like Swiss cheese, riddled with holes and tunnels. It was a place where the spirits of the old ones still roamed, you could feel them. Their presence was all around us. Suddenly, the fact that I was holding a gun on Tate made me feel as if I were violating something sacred. There almost seemed to be voices on the wind, or maybe it was just the coyotes. They sounded the same to me.

Tate heard it too and called over her shoulder. "Pop always told me that was the sound of the old ones who used to live here. Here, look." She pointed to several large, round circles still evident in the desert floor. "Tepee rings," she explained. "A Sioux tribe called this home over five hundred years ago."

I stopped and stared as my past reared up, and suddenly I was overcome by a very real feeling of being observed. I think Dakota felt it too. Mom had told us about our Indian heritage all our lives, but growing up in a predominantly white community, I never knew what that meant until that moment. My ancestors had lived here, *here,* in this place. I had no doubt they were watching me now, judging me, deeming me worthy of being in this holy place. I knew in my heart I was not.

"Pretty powerful, huh?" Tate said when she saw our reaction. "Well, you haven't seen anything yet. Come on."

She led us past the tepee rings and around a high rock formation that could have passed for a chimney. It looked like all that was left of a house that had burned down.

"You have to duck a little here," she said. Moving under a natural rock bridge that spanned a gap between two more spiraling towers, she squatted down and entered what looked like a small oblong hole into the side of a solid rock face.

When Dakota and I just stood there watching where she'd disappeared, she poked her head back out looking for us.

"You've got to be kidding," Dakota said.

"Come on, tough guy," she said. "*I'm going to shoot you or leave you, I haven't decided which.* Please!" Tate started to laugh as she made fun of Dakota. "It's a little tight for a few feet, but then it widens out, trust me." She turned back around and disappeared once more.

"She wants us to trust her," I said to Dakota.

"Isn't she the one who wanted to run us out of town?" he asked me.

I just shrugged and bent down. At first the hole looked too small to accommodate me, but I found if I put my arms out in front of me, it narrowed my shoulders enough to just squeeze through. Tate wasn't kidding when she said it was a tight fit. It was, I imagined, much like the passageway that brought us into this world. The top of the tunnel just brushed my head and surrounded me on both sides. I was grateful that claustrophobia was not one of my weaknesses.

The rock was cold, there was no light and very little air. Dirt clogged my nostrils, and my muscles cramped from trying to fit through a place not designed to accommodate my bulk. I was not a five-feet-two inch, one-hundred-and-ten-pound woman. Just as I thought I might have to wiggle back out again, the tunnel suddenly widened into a voluminous cave. The ceiling vaulted at least ten feet above my head and had a diameter of eighty feet or more. A natural hole in the rock formation above us let in fresh air and light. The red of the stone gave a warm, almost welcoming hue to the cave where the sun streaked through and painted the sides in bright slashes of light.

The tunnel exited about four feet off the ground. Going through headfirst, I had no choice but to drop down that way. Rolling to my feet, I shook the dirt out of my hair and brushed it from my clothes. Didn't do much good. Turning in a small circle, I surveyed the place. There were smaller caves and tunnels branching out from this one. A maze within a maze. I heard Dakota struggle through the opening and gave him a hand down. His reaction mirrored my own. He circled me, his dirt-streaked face lifted to the heights, taking it all in.

"Wow," he said, his voice echoing off the walls.

"Pretty amazing, I know," Tate said.

"You found this place when you were ten?" I asked.

"Yeah, it seemed a lot bigger back then." She smiled.

"What on earth made you even want to go into that tunnel?" I asked. "It just looks like a depression from the outside."

"I rode out here after school one day and it started to rain, I mean pour, a real drencher. I looked for a place to wait it out and thought the hole would offer at least a little protection. It wasn't until after I poked my head in I found it was a tunnel. My curiosity got the better of me and I followed it. It wasn't long after that I found the treasure room."

"Treasure room?" Dakota asked.

Tate grinned. "Well, that's what I called it when I was ten. The name stuck, I guess. Come on, but I gotta' warn you, you might find this a little weird. I mean, I didn't put it all together until after we talked last night, and even than I wasn't sure."

"What are you talking about?" I asked her.

"Just look. Oh wait, you'll need this." She handed me a kerosene lantern obviously brought in on one of her visits. Opening up a tin can next to it, she pulled out a pack of matches and handed them to me. "No natural lighting in there," she explained.

Dakota and I exchanged confused glances as I lit the lantern. The harsh smell of kerosene filled the air. Tate led us to one of the larger tunnels branching off from the main room. It was small by comparison, but still held both of us comfortably, even if we did have to duck to accommodate the lower ceiling.

The first thing I noticed was the drawings on the walls. I thought they were ancient Indian pictographs, but then I realized the paint was modern. Oils or some type of acrylic, I wasn't sure which, but definitely not berries and crushed rock. The next thing I noticed was that the subject in every painting was the same. A woman. A very beautiful Native woman. In some she was naked and the poses were almost erotic, in others she smiled coyly at the painter, her long straight dark hair falling across half her face. She looked like a woman in love.

The progression of the paintings seemed to follow a timeline of sorts. The woman was seen in different important stages in her life. One painting simply showed two hands, one laid on top of the other, a beaded ceremonial cord wrapped around them, one hand female, the other male. Another naked painting, this time the woman was shown obviously pregnant, her hands caressing her protruding abdomen, her head flung back in joy as if she was laughing. There were several more of just her face, painted in incredible rich detail. I passed the light quickly over these when Dakota stopped me.

"Wait," he said, his voice low, but seemingly too loud in the confines of the small cave. "Go back to the last few, the paintings of just her face," he requested.

I did and he leaned in close, taking the lantern from me and studying the series of portraits in silence. All that could be heard was the quiet hiss of the lantern and our own breathing. Dakota, finally having found what he was looking for, pulled back and looked at me. Confusion played across his face. It looked as if he was trying to convince himself of something that made no sense.

"Montana," he said, wiping sweat from his face with the sleeve of his shirt. It left a streak of mud in its place. "Those are paintings of Mom," he said with absolute confidence.

I shook my head. "What?" I leaned in with the light much as he had done and still refused to see it. "No, no way, Dak. All Native woman have similar features, could be anyone. I mean, grant you, I can see a resemblance, but that is not our mother."

I was absolutely convinced of that right up to the point where he centered the light at the end of the trail of paintings where the artist had signed his work. It was written in Sioux, a language my mother had taken great pains to teach us. Neither of us could be considered fluent, but I knew enough to translate the few lines written in bold script on the rock face.

And ever has it been known that love knows not its own depth until the hour of separation. Forever Lilly. I miss you, Jacob.

"None of this makes sense," I said, still refusing to believe what I was looking at.

"There's more," Tate said from just outside.

I panned the light across the floor and found tin after tin stacked around the sides. They were covered in dust and rusted. It was obvious no one had touched them in quite some time.

"What's in them?" I asked her.

"Pictures mostly, a couple of letters, a child's drawing. I looked once and felt as if I was violating his privacy. So I just made sure they were safe, took them home with me once when the *rohos* flooded."

I still didn't understand, or maybe I didn't want to. I returned my attention back to the dust-covered tins. I held the light up as Dakota bent down to open one.

Old black and white photographs mixed with colored digital prints filled the canister. I picked one up at random and felt the immediate need to sit down. In the picture was a man, a Native man. His black hair was long, *just like the old ones,* it had been a windy day, his hair caught up in the breeze, obscuring most of his face. He was smiling and looking with complete adoration at the child sitting on his lap. The child, a boy of maybe one or two, played with a necklace around the man's neck, a turquoise fetish of a coyote howling.

Reaching under my dirt-streaked shirt, I pulled out the only piece of jewelry I ever wore. It was a gift given to me by my mother when I was fifteen. She told me it had belonged to my father. I looked at the turquoise fetish fashioned in the shape of a howling coyote strung on a leather cord. I treasured the thing as my only physical connection to my father, I never took it off.

Staring at the man's face in the picture, I realized that I was now sitting on the dirt floor, my knees having given out on me. My heart was trying to convince my mind of the something I struggled to accept.

In my hands I held a picture of my father who in turn held me as a child. He was real, and I now had proof of it. Dakota had been doing his own looking and handed me a professional quality family portrait. If I had any doubts they were extinguished then. I looked at a very young, very beautiful Lilly Thomas standing next to my father. My mother held an infant in her arms, Dakota, and my father held me on his hip. One happy family, smiling for the camera. A moment frozen in time that I would have given anything to remember.

Still holding the photographs, I raised the light to gaze on my father's renditions of my mother. I turned to Tate who had bent down next to me.

"You knew, didn't you?" I asked her.

"I guessed. When you told me your father's name was Jacob, I thought there might be a connection, but I wasn't sure until I found you in the tombs."

I shook my head, still confused. "I don't get it," I said, thinking that was an understatement. "Why did you freak? What scared you so much that you thought you needed to make us leave, that you wanted us to believe our lives were in danger if we stayed?"

Tate sat down next to me and reached inside her shirt. "Because your life is in danger, both of you." She pulled out a necklace of her own, it was nearly identical to mine. A howling coyote fetish on a leather thong.

"A gift from *my* father," she told me. Leaning past me, she grabbed a box we had yet to open, placed the tin on her lap and searched through the pictures, obviously looking for one particular shot.

"I thought you said you only looked at these once," I said.

"Once was all it took," she said, finding what she was looking for and holding the desired picture close to her chest. "You see, I found something out when I was ten years old that should have been kept a secret. Something I was never meant to know. At first I believed I found this Jacob's secret place, his place of remembrance. I didn't come back for a long time after that first day, convinced he would be angry that someone had found him out, but I couldn't stay away. The secret was too big, and I had no one to share it with."

"You didn't tell your father?" I asked.

She shook her head. "I didn't think he would understand." She laughed at her own words. "Anyway, I placed little trip wires over the tunnel, I wanted to see if he had come back. After months of him being a no show, I decided he wasn't coming back and took it upon myself to watch over his memories. That's when I opened the picture tins for the first time. Even at ten I knew."

She held out the photograph to me. I took it from her, and both Dakota and I looked at the image printed on the paper. It was a later shot, the man had cut his hair. The pieces of the puzzle started to fall into place.

"Do you see?" she asked me, the tears spilling over her lashes. "Now do you understand?"

I studied the picture closely. I saw a slightly older version of Jacob Willowcreek, and when I looked again I could see why Tate was crying.

"Jacob Willowcreek and my father David Willows are the same person," Tate said. "I knew it when I was ten. I spent so many hours trying to figure out who Lilly was, I was jealous of someone I never met, jealous that someone, *anyone,* could bring that kind of emotion out of my father. He has always been so guarded, so closed off. I could never figure out why, but I knew this Lilly had something to do with the sadness he showed to the world."

Even though I knew the truth behind her words, they were a physical slap. My mind backtracked over the last twenty-four hours, and settled on the conversation I had on the deck with David. I had met my father, I had spoken with him, and I never even knew it.

CHAPTER 13

"Why?" Dakota asked, taking the picture from me.

"Why what?" Tate turned her head to watch Dakota. "Why did he turn himself into someone else? Why didn't he tell me or my mother about Lilly? Why did he leave two sons and never look back?"

Dakota handed the photo back to her. "All good questions, but no. Why did you think it was necessary to chase us out of town, why all the cloak and dagger? I mean, shooting up a library? That's a little extreme, don't you think?"

Tate shrugged. "Listen to what I found out today, and then you tell me."

"Thought you had a test today," I said.

She turned her blue eyes in my direction and gave me a scowl. "Yeah, I thought saving your ass may be a bit more important."

"What did you find?" I asked her, ignoring the comment.

"A death certificate for Jacob Willowcreek. And another one for David Willowcreek."

"Oh my God," I said finally getting it.

"What?" Dakota asked, his eyes going from me to Tate and back again.

Tate stared at me, the reality of what she had been carrying for the last few hours finally breaking her. Tears filled her eyes and she looked for comfort somewhere, anywhere. I pulled her into my arms and offered her what I could. Silent sobs tore through her as she allowed herself to let it go. I held her and found Dakota looking back at me in confusion.

"What?" he asked again.

Looking at him over Tate's head, I told him, "Jacob faked his own death. I don't know why or how, but when he did, he left us and created a new identity for himself. David Willowcreek, AKA David Willows. Either a brother or a relative." Pulling back, I asked Tate for confirmation of that fact.

Sniffling and wiping her face on my shirt, she nodded. "Brother," she told me. "He died in infancy. Your Jacob took his identity and made a new life for himself. He became David Willows and moved here to hide from a past he thought he needed to run from."

"The question I want an answer to, is why?" I asked.

"Your Jacob Willowcreek liked to gamble," she said. Maybe it was easier for her to accept what she had learned about the man who had raised her if she thought of him as two separate entities. Her father and our Jacob. "At the time of his 'death' he was in debt up to his gonads."

"Maybe he thought he had no choice but to run," I said.

"That's what I thought too," Tate said. "But then I accessed his income tax records for the last few years."

"You can do that?" Dakota asked. He looked as if he still hadn't gotten around the fact that our father had faked his own death.

"Piece of cake." Tate gave him a small smile. "Anyway, his records for the last five years of his life show an income barely above the poverty level. Then the year he disappeared, that all changed. He listed his income as more than ten million dollars. He paid his taxes, and then he died. Two years later he shows up in Ekalaka, only now he's David

Willows. He met and married my mother and created an entirely new existence, a new life, complete with a new family."

"Still doesn't explain why you believed our lives were in danger, why you thought you needed to scare us away," Dakota said, trying to figure it out.

"Yes, it does." I turned to my brother and pulled out the copy of the canceled check still in my pocket. "Now we know where Mom got the half a mil. Jake's income goes from the poverty level to over ten million in one year. I don't think he won the lottery, Dakota."

"He was skimming?" Dakota asked.

"Well, he was doing something, and whoever he did it to obviously wasn't very happy about it," Tate chimed in.

"We need to talk to David Willows, too many unanswered questions," I said.

"I think you're forgetting something," Tate reminded us.

"And what would that be?" I asked her.

"If Jacob Willowcreek ran because he stole that money, whoever it belonged to would have been pissed as hell, pissed enough to kill. Maybe that's why he ran, maybe that's why he's been hiding all these years. Now you two come into town and are sitting right on his doorstep, asking questions and stirring up a lot of unwanted attention. You tell me, if someone stole that much money from you, would you ever stop looking?"

"We might have led them right to him," Dakota said, finally understanding.

I understood why Tate feared for our lives as well.

"Or you led them to the next best thing. Whoever is still looking for your father might just settle for his sons. A little blood debt that has waited a very long time to be paid."

It made sense. It was why our mother had chosen an English name for us to bear. Why she never had any contact with her family or her culture, and why for all the times I ever asked her, she never told me about my father. Lilly Thomas did what any mother would have done. She was protecting her children the only way she knew how. She was following the wishes of a man who loved her and his family enough to disappear from their lives just to keep them safe.

* * * *

The drive back to Willow Run was made in silence. Tate sat up front with me, and Dakota volunteered to take the back. He had said very little since we discovered the truth about David Willows. Dakota never spoke much about our father, and I'd always been too wrapped up in my own obsession about the man to think to ask him. He was the one who took Mom's side, the one who went looking for me when we were kids. He took my abuse and stood by me, always he stood by me. I knew now I was wrong to misinterpret that loyalty as understanding. I don't think Dakota ever understood why I could never just let it alone, why I always had to push it. I remember he asked me once when we were maybe ten and eleven. *Why can't you just take what you have? Why do you always have to want more?*

At eleven I failed to hear the pain in his words, the need in him for us to simply be the family we could be. My answer to him was typical and a mindset that I had yet to change. *Because I deserve more.*

I never once stopped to consider how my actions affected him. Watching him through the rearview mirror, I saw the same look on his face as I saw back then. My gut clenched, wondering what he might be thinking. With Tate in the car, it was not the time to ask him. I wasn't sure he would talk to me if we were alone either.

I pulled into the long drive and Tate turned to me. "Do you want to talk to him first, or do you want me to say something?"

I shook my head. "No, don't say anything."

She looked as exhausted as I felt. Finding the secrets you've searched a lifetime for can have that effect on you.

"I wouldn't know what to say anyway." She got out the car, looked around the property and then at her watch. "You might find him out in the garden, around the house in the back."

I nodded and got out of the Jeep, looking at her over the roof. The reality of everything hit as our eyes locked. The attraction we felt toward one another from the beginning was still there, but now it was something untouchable. It was hard to look at her with the afternoon sun glinting off her black hair, her blue eyes brimming with tears. All I wanted to do was walk around the Jeep and hold her.

Tate seemed to realize what I was thinking and shook her head and ran inside the house, tears falling down her face.

Dakota got out of the backseat and started walking down the driveway.

"Where you going?" I called after him.

"I need some air," he yelled back without turning around to look at me.

"Something wrong with the air right here?" I asked, hoping to elicit a smart-ass remark from him, my barometer for how he was feeling.

Dakota ignored the remark and kept walking steadily down the drive. Definitely not a good sign, but I could only handle one personal crisis at a time. I would let Dakota have his air, Tate could have her space, and David Willows? I thought it might be time for the man to meet his son.

I walked around to the back of the house and scanned the area, looking for some sign of Dave Willows. I wanted to see him face to face, I needed to find out if what I had seen in the pictures was true. I pulled the print I found in the cave from my jacket pocket and tried to convince myself that moment in time had actually existed once. I was that child and the man who held me, my father. My hand went to the fetish around my neck as I pondered the question. I gripped the cool stone and tried to convince myself this was a good thing—the answers to a lifetime were within my reach. Why then, did I hesitate? Why was I still so furious?

A part of me was relieved to find the yard empty, the other part frustrated by the delay. A movement off to one side of the house caught my attention and I noticed a storage shed there. The door opened and a wheelbarrow emerged, pushed out the opening by David. I stepped back into the shadows and observed the man with the knowledge that I was indeed looking at my father. *My father!* That simple fact paralyzed me. How could I not have seen it before? His movements, the way he held his body, the tilt of his head as he went about his tasks, I recognized them as my own.

This is what I had wanted since I was four years old, to meet my father. He was less than ten feet away, and I couldn't move. All I ever concentrated on was finding the man. I never gave any thought as to what I might say to him once I did. Not really. I would strut and tell him off in front of my mirror as a kid, but it was just a show. Maybe a part of me was certain this day would never happen. I watched my father and had no idea what to do next.

My body seemed to move of its own accord. Leaving the shadows, I walked toward David as he shoveled compost from the wheelbarrow into a plot of recently plowed earth. His back was turned to me and my approach had been silent. I stopped about five feet away and just watched him. He was still in good shape, the thin cotton shirt he wore was covered in sweat and gave testament to a body that had not forgotten hard work.

I don't know how long I stood there, trying to figure out what to say, trying to remember all the speeches I had devised over the years, all the words I would so eloquently throw at him when I met him. My mind went blank. I almost turned around and left when I saw him stop in mid-shovel.

"You just going to keep standing there watching me, or are you going to help?" he asked.

I peeled off my jacket, picked up an extra shovel lying nearby and started shoveling compost. There was a certain symmetry about that. Without looking at him I started to talk, it was easier that way.

"How long have you known?" I asked him. I wiped sweat out of my eyes with the back of one hand and waited for his answer.

David shrugged, his muscles bunching under the weight of the shovel. "From the first night. I watched you get out of that Jeep and walk up my porch steps, and I knew." Pushing the shovel into the pile of compost spread out around his feet, he leaned on the handle and looked at me for the first time. "Dakota has the old man's eyes," he said.

"He didn't seem to care for you very much," I said. "The old man," I clarified.

"Yeah, I know."

"I looked for you almost all my life." The words spilled out of me uncensored. I wanted to take them back the moment they were out.

"I know." He nodded, his gaze settling just ahead of us, focusing on nothing. "I'm sorry."

His admission took me by surprise. "You knew?"

"Caliente is small, but it's not invisible. I had a copy of the daily paper sent to a post office box in Wyoming. From there it was mailed to another PO box in Billings. I would pay a local college kid to pick it up and drive it to me once a month. You drove poor Cal crazy." He smiled and it was like looking in a mirror.

The anger that had driven me all of my life came to a head as I listened to him make light of a childhood spent in turmoil all because of what he had done. Dropping the shovel, I went with the feeling. Tired of holding the rage in, tired of keeping that part of me under the surface and showing a different face to everyone else. I let the leash slip and let the monster out his cage for a brief moment.

"You son-of-a-bitch." I glared at him. "You broke her heart, you broke *her.* She used to take me out to the desert at night, to listen for you. Those damn Lakota legends." The anger built up inside me. I wanted to let it take over this time. "She told me that you were a coyote spirit. She would sit in the desert and listen for them, for *you* to talk to her. *That* was my childhood. A mother who balanced on the edge of sanity, sitting in the desert at night listening to the coyotes sing. Now here you are making light of what drove me to look for you, to find a father who my mother refused to acknowledge as anything other than a story."

David had the decency to look ashamed. "I'm sorry," he said again.

I was in no mood for an apology. The words meant to soothe sent me over the edge. "Too little, too late." I took two quick steps to bridge the distance between us, then pulled back my fist and let it go.

The blow caught him just under his left eye and sent him flying. He landed on his back, his hand rubbing his face.

"Can't say I didn't deserve that."

It wasn't the response I expected, and it totally deflated my anger.

"That's it?" I asked, circling around his still supine form. "You're not going to fight back? You're not going to defend yourself?" I wanted him to get up. I wanted him to throw a punch so I could beat the shit out of the man and justify it by saying it was self-defense.

"Now why would I do that?" He smiled at me as he got to his feet. "Just to give you an excuse to wail on me?" He rubbed his cheek. "No, thanks. I owed you one free punch, after that…" He shrugged.

"Do you know she's dead?" I asked. I wanted to hurt him, I wanted him to feel a piece of the pain he had caused me my entire life. I thought if I threw my mother's death in his face, I might achieve that. The look on his face told me I did.

"I know. Sam Blackcrow has my cellphone number. He told me you popped in on the old man, told me about Lilly." His voiced cracked as he said my mother's name.

"I knew that old man wasn't telling us everything," I said.

David shook his head. "Well, to be fair, he never told me he sent you here. Guess he thought I deserved a little surprise of my own."

"I don't even know what to call you," I admitted.

My anger gone for the moment, I motioned to where I had hit him. He tenderly touched the area under his left eye. It was already beginning to swell.

"You should probably get some ice on that."

He nodded in agreement. "Nice right hook. Why don't we go inside? It's cooler, and I know you have questions. Besides, I think I could use a drink." The flash of a smile was back and he headed for the door.

I followed him into the kitchen and went to the freezer. I cracked open an ice cube tray, emptied the contents into a kitchen towel, twisted it closed, then handed it to him. "Drinks" turned out to be a fifth of Johnnie Walker. He poured two shots, and I gratefully downed one. It burned wonderfully on the way down, sitting warm and happy in my gut. I took a second and finally thought I had enough courage to ask the one question I had asked countless times alone in the dark. The only difference was this time I expected an answer.

"Why, Jacob?" I asked. "Why?"

Taking the towel full of ice, he held it gingerly over his rapidly swelling eye and shook his head. "David, please, it's David now."

I gave him that small measure and waited for an answer.

"I met Lilly Longfoot when I was twenty-three years old. She was seventeen, and I have never seen a more beautiful sight. I never will." He closed his eyes, lost in the memory for a moment.

I wished I could have seen what he was seeing. But then he opened his eyes and the past was the past again. All that existed was the present and a story he needed to tell a son he had only just met.

"I knew I loved her from the first time I spoke with her. I know how that sounds, but it's the truth. It was the same for her." He sighed, and then put that behind him as well.

"I was passing through the Dakotas. I had business at the casinos in Montana and Nevada, not Las Vegas, but the Native casinos off the main strip. I was pretty good at cards, blackjack and roulette. Won more times than I ever lost. Thought maybe I could earn some money at it. Not gambling, but working there, as a dealer or later on maybe as a pit boss. I never counted on falling in love.

"I couldn't leave her, and all she wanted was to be with me. I tried to make it right with Joseph. But he was being stubborn. Lilly might have been young, but she always knew what she wanted and would stop at nothing to get it." He paused in his story and looked up at me. "It was her, you have to believe that. I was leaving without her, didn't want too, but I promised her I would be back. Found her curled up in the backseat of my car. Said she was going with me, would die if I left her there. I loved her, and she had tears in her eyes, and she was begging me to take her with me. Maybe I wasn't as strong as I should have been, should have taken her back, but I didn't."

"It didn't turn out quite like you expected though," I said.

He shook his head. "No, does it ever?" Then answering his own question, he continued his story. "I did find work, but as a part of the housekeeping staff. We cleaned up after everyone left for the day. The money I made was barely enough to pay for rent, let alone food and utilities." He ran a hand through his hair, a gesture I recognized as one of my own. "Then we found out she was pregnant. I knew I had to do something. I went to the manager and told them I was good with numbers, told them I would do anything, I had a family to feed. I knew I sounded desperate, I didn't care."

"What happen?"

"He asked me how serious I was about doing anything, told me he would see to it that my family would be well taken care of, I would never want for money again. That's when he showed me the books."

"The books?"

"You have to understand, this was before computers, before the internet. Everything was written down and filed away. His previous accountant had been an old and trusted friend, emphasis on 'old'. He died about a month before and they had yet to replace him. I think they were almost as desperate as I was. He gave me more money than I had ever seen—in cash—told me it was an advance, to take the day off, go home and think about it and let him know in the morning."

"What did he want you to do, Dad?" I realized it was the first time I addressed him as my father. I didn't mean to, it just happened, and it was too late to take it back even if I wanted to. I wasn't sure I did.

David couldn't look at me, he watched his hands instead. "The casino was keeping two sets of books, one they showed the IRS, the other that showed what they really made. Bottom line—the Native casinos are supposed to donate a portion of what they make to the local reservations for college funds, things our people would not be able to afford normally. The casinos were making almost triple the profit they reported. They wanted me to keep the books, both sets, and they would pay me more money than I had ever dreamed of to keep their secret."

"And if you refused?" I knew the answer to that question, but needed to hear it anyway.

"They would kill me and my family." He finally managed to meet my eyes. "I didn't have a choice."

"How long did you work for them?" I kept my face neutral, but inside I was torn. My father had betrayed his own people to feed his children. Would I have done any different?

"Almost two years." He looked away again. "That's when I decided I couldn't do it anymore. I knew how they operated now, it would be easy. I made a third book—my book. I skimmed the profits they were taking from the education funds, set up a separate account under a false identity, and I took the money." He gave me a sideways glance, his eyes filled with shame. "It was a lot of money, Montana."

"They found out." It wasn't a question.

"I should have left that night, but I thought it would look too suspicious, so I just kept doing my job. That's when it all went wrong. I don't know how, but they figured it out. They didn't find my books, but they managed to trace the missing money back to me.

"Dakota was only a few weeks old when they found me at home with Lilly. They sent hired muscle in an attempt to make me give them their money back. But they weren't as dumb as they looked. They never laid a hand on me. They went straight for Lilly." He squeezed his eyes tightly together, as if by doing so he could change the past. I wondered how many times he relived that one moment in his life.

"What happened?" I asked, wanting to know, needing to know, and at the same time afraid to hear the words.

David took a deep breath and relived his own personal hell. "There were five of them. Took three of them to hold me down, while the other two beat Lilly. They took the baby and put him in his bassinet and shut you in your room, then made me watch while they beat her half to death."

He shook his head, his eyes brimming with things he had buried too deep for too long. But it was clear the burden he was forced to carry was more than any one man was ever meant to take. He made sure he had my complete attention before he went on, the pain of that day still fresh and vivid on his face as he spoke of it.

"They told me unless the money was returned to a numbered account they gave me, they would come back for the kids, maybe break one of your arms, maybe even kill you. The things they told me they would do to Lilly, I can't even tell you. I had one week. If the money wasn't returned by then they would come back and make good on their threats. Me, they would let live, at least until after they killed everyone I cared about. But I knew they wouldn't leave it at that. Even if I returned every cent. It was too late anyway, I had already given most of it to the Lakota council, which is where it should've gone to begin with."

"The bruises Joseph saw on her," I said more to myself than to David. "He thought you were beating her."

He nodded. "I sent her back to him with you and Dakota. I had to move fast. She took another name and traveled under it. No one knew where Lilly came from, her last name. We were never officially married, just handfasted, it was enough for us. She left in the middle of the night. I told her to stay there. The money I had left I hid in several secured accounts under her new name. Some I kept. Lilly would never have to worry about money as long as she lived. I could hide her, I could hide the money, but if I stayed with her I ran the risk of her and my children being hurt, maybe even killed." He looked up at me, his face tortured. "They would have killed you, you have to believe that. You and Dakota were the only two things I ever got right in my whole life. If it meant never seeing you again to keep you safe, then that's what I would do."

Emotions threatened to overwhelm him and he took a moment. I let him.

When he spoke again, he was calmer. "I wish I had it to do all over again. When I took Lilly to Montana for the first time, I brought her to Medicine Rocks." He smiled at the memory. Seventeen years old and she had seen nothing but the small, God-forsaken town she had grown up in. She was so sheltered, so innocent. Everything delighted her. It was night and she walked up to the big monolith in the center of the formations. She put her hands on the rock and told me she knew this place was alive." David put the towel full of ice down on the table, his skin red and swollen either from the cold or the punch. "She told me she could feel them, the ancient ones, she could feel their presence in the rock. I believed she really could."

He smiled, his eyes alive with a past he didn't seem to visit very often. He blinked and came back to the present when he looked at me.

"When you were born, she knew that was where you were conceived and was adamant about naming you Montana." David shrugged almost in apology. "I'm sure you know what it's like to try to talk Lilly out of something she wants."

I laughed. "You didn't have a chance in hell."

His face turned sad again. "No, I didn't. I had three years with her. *Three years!* You had nearly thirty, I envy you."

"Envy Dakota," I said. "I spent the majority of that time being so angry at her we barely spoke for the last ten years."

"Over me," he said, understanding.

"She kept your secret well."

"I'm sorry."

I was still angry, but it didn't seem as important now. "It was my choice. You did what you thought you had to, and I guess I did the same."

"You were everything to me, you and Dakota. I need you to believe that."

"I'll see what I can do about that." It was the best I could do at the moment.

"You were two the last time I saw you. I sat you on my lap and you played with a fetish I used to wear, you were fascinated by the little thing. I don't know why, but I always remembered that. I told you I needed to go away and you needed to take care of mom and your brother. Do you remember what you said?"

"I was two," I reminded him.

"Yeah, I just remember how mature you seemed at the time and I always wondered if you would remember."

"What did I say?" I touched the fetish resting beneath my shirt. I wondered if I should give it back or keep it hidden. I removed my hand and kept my secret.

"You looked up at me and told me that you would protect me. That I shouldn't worry about the bad men, because you were going to take care of them all. You saw," he said, tears spilling over black lashes. "You were only two years old and you witnessed those bastards beat your mother while they made me watch. There you were trying to make it all better for me." He wiped viciously at the tears as if they should have asked permission to be there. "God, do you have any idea how that made me feel? As a father? As a man? My two-year-old wanted to protect me. No one was going to make you feel like that ever again and if it took me disappearing from Lilly's life to do that, than that is what I would do."

"I spent a lifetime trying to figure out what I would say to you if I ever got the chance. The intent changed as I got older, but for the most part, I wanted to hate you for what you did to our mother, for not being there for me, for us," I said.

"I'm not asking for your forgiveness, Montana. I know it's too late for that."

"Then what do you want from me?"

"Understanding, maybe," he said.

I motioned up the stairs. "What about Tate? Just how does she fit into all of this? Is she just cover? Did you use her and her mother just to complete the perfect picture of the happy family?"

"That's not fair," David said. "I love Tate, I loved her mother,"

"I thought you said Lilly was the love of your life," I goaded him.

"She was, but I couldn't have her. I'm not a saint, Montana. I'm human, I wanted companionship."

I thought about my mother and the stories she used to cling on to her sanity. The tales she spun for a little boy who only wanted the truth. Now the truth stared me in the face, and it still wasn't good enough. I tried to control the anger, but the words came out on their own accord. "So, any port in a storm, is that how it works?"

"You're out of line, Montana," he warned me. "Jillian never knew about Lilly, there was no need for it. I loved her as well as I could."

"And Tate, what was she, a pale substitute for two sons?"

"I will allow that, because I know you feel the need to hurt me, but no more, understand?"

"Or what, you'll send me to my room? Sorry *Dad* but you missed out on that privilege about twenty years ago."

"I think you need to cool off a little. Why don't you go for a walk or something?" David suggested.

"Yeah, maybe I do. Maybe I'll drive back to Medicine Rocks, to the cave where you painted my mother, where you professed your love for her."

The look of complete confusion on his face was exactly what I wanted to see.

"Yeah, I know about your little secret, and guess who showed me?

Tate has known about your double life since she was ten years old, *Dave*." I felt the monster gathering strength and knew I needed to get some serious distance between me and my father or one of us would end up with a hell of a lot more than a black eye.

I walked out of the kitchen, nabbing the bottle of scotch on the way, and headed toward the back yard, where I first found my father. In a moment of unparalleled anger, I pulled the coyote fetish from around my neck, snapping the leather cord that held it there. I held it in my fist, fully intending to throw this one connection to my father into the abyss, but I couldn't do it. I just couldn't do it. Instead I threw the necklace on the compost pile and wondered if David would understand the silent message I was sending him.

I was giving him back that part he had given me almost twenty-seven years ago. I didn't want it anymore.

I was hoping to hurt him. It was childish and stupid, but I did it anyway. I left Dakota, Tate and Jacob Willowcreek, got in my Jeep and just drove. The direction didn't matter. It was the distance that mattered.

I was twenty-nine years old and I was running away again.

CHAPTER 14

It was dusk, and I was a little surprised when I found myself back at Medicine Rocks. Maybe surprised wasn't the right word, I felt drawn to the place from the first moment Tate had shown it to me. The sun was dropping behind the hills fast, and I had only moments of daylight left. I'd parked the Jeep in the back of the parking lot and walked the distance to the rocks without thinking of bringing a flashlight with me. I glanced up to the darkening sky and saw the gathering clouds. The walk back to my Jeep would be one in darkness if not in rain.

The last rays of sunlight played over the huge sandstone. I pulled my jacket on as I realized the temperature had dropped significantly in the last few minutes. It left me shivering, as much as the conversation with my father had left me unsettled.

My anger and frustration faded, leaving me with a vague numbness and fatigue. It isn't every day you learn the secrets of a lifetime. It was enough to leave anyone feeling a little off balance. Or maybe it was the scotch. I wasn't a drinker, never liked the stuff. I was what Dakota called a cheap date. I laughed at the thought as I raised the bottle to my lips and took another healthy swig. The bitter liquid felt oddly comforting, my head had a fuzzy, heavy feeling that was not at all unwelcome. I didn't want to think, just this once, I didn't want to have to confront the demons alone.

The demons had one hell of a sense of humor.

I heard the slide of a weapon pulled back a half a second before I recognized what was happening. I was unarmed, and I was working up a good drunk. Like shooting carnival ducks. Without looking behind me, I dropped the bottle and dove for cover underneath one of the outcroppings of rock creating the unusual features of the landmark. The spray of bullets erupted around me, and I heard the gunman drop his empty clip and reload. In the few moments I was allowed, I pushed to my feet and ran for deeper cover. A vision of Tate firing at us in the library crossed my mind and was immediately dismissed. Whoever was shooting at me was a trained marksman. The shots were tight and uncomfortably close. These were not meant to scare, somebody wanted me hurt or dead.

Another volley of shots, I recognized the sound of the weapon as a semi-automatic, I also knew they were coming from closer than the first round. Either there was more than one gunman or they knew where I was.

Night vision? That thought scared me more than the threat of multiple bad guys. Night vision implied professionals. *Who the hell did you piss off, Dad?*

The impending rain clouds left the night without benefit of moon or stars, good news for me as long as the guy with the gun didn't have any toys, like night vision or infrared scopes.

I heard another clip drop and knew I only had seconds to decide what to do. I tried to orient myself as to where I was in reference to Tate's cave. God! I had to pick today for my drinking debut. Despite the adrenaline that zinged through my system, my head was still fuzzed. Nothing looked familiar. If I could get to the cave without whoever was out there hearing me, I thought I might have a chance, *if* they were alone, *if* they didn't have night vision, and *if* I could remember in which direction it lay. I wasn't having a good day.

I squeezed my eyes shut for a second at my own stupidity, and then fear made an appearance. I didn't like that. If whoever was out there in the dark knew enough to follow me, then they already knew who I was and most likely knew who David Willows was as well. That meant not only was my father's life in danger, so were Dakota's and Tate's, and there wasn't a damn thing I could do to protect them.

Lightning flashed behind the distant hills, and thunder rumbled across the desert floor a moment later. A storm was coming. I looked for some sign of the gunman in the momentary flash. I needn't have bothered.

I felt the cold barrel of a weapon pressed against the back of my skull a moment before I heard the round chambered. I was off my game.

"Don't even twitch."

Since I was already on the ground, I held my hands out to my sides, showing him I was unarmed.

"Check him," the gunman instructed.

Two of them.

The other one pushed me flat to the ground and kicked my legs apart, then kneeling on the small of my back, he none-too-gently searched me for concealed weapons.

"He's clean," the searcher told the gunman.

"Which one are you?" the gunman asked me.

The question took me off guard for a moment, and I was suddenly reminded of my grandfather asking me the same question.

"Does it matter?" I was rewarded for my sarcasm by having the butt of the gun slammed against the back of my head. A brilliant flash of light that wasn't lightning exploded behind my eyes, and a searing pain followed a moment after that. I felt the searcher go for the wallet at my hip and waited for my head to clear.

"Montana Lee Thomas," Searcher told Gunman.

Gunman gave a satisfied grunt. "Been looking for you, boy."

"Found me." I knew I should've just shut up, but what the hell, if they were going to kill me anyway I was going to go out my way. I felt blood, warm and thick, flow down the back of my neck and my eyes blurred. "Is it my turn to be 'it' now?" I asked.

Searcher's boot found my ribs. I grunted with the pain as bone gave way and snapped under the assault. I curled into a ball, trying to get my breath back and fight the waves of nausea that attacked. Not even Johnnie Walker was going to numb this.

"Apparently not," I said as I drew in a painful breath.

Gunman bent down and rolled me over so I faced him. He put the gun in my face and pulled me up by my shirt so we were nose to nose. I could smell sweat and onions on him. They had waited for me, until they could get me alone. They had sat in the dark and ate while they waited. The waiting was over. Now they were going to have fun.

"Your mama was tougher than you, boy," Gunman said, as Searcher snickered. "That was one pretty little squaw who knew how to put up a fight."

That was probably the only thing that could have made me forget the pain. Gunman didn't expect me to lunge for the weapon that was only inches from my face. I grabbed it with both hands and pushed it to the side. We struggled for the weapon, the adrenaline that had given me momentary strength quickly fading as my broken ribs ripped and tore at flesh.

Searcher came to his partner's aid and once again kicked me. This time the target was my hip, just above my pelvis. Despite the new pain blossoming there, I still wouldn't relinquish my hold on the gun. I knew if I left go, I was dead.

Gunman put an end to the struggle. His finger found the trigger first, and he didn't hesitate to pull it.

The struggle had ruined his aim, the bullet hit me just below my left shoulder in my upper arm. The pain was incredible. I immediately let go of the gun, my right hand instinctively clamping over the bleeding wound.

Gunman was pissed now. "You son-of-a-bitch!" He grabbed a handful of hair and yanked my head back until I was forced to look at him. "I watched you watching me as I beat your mama, boy. You were only one or two, but I knew you hated me." He grinned at me. The man who had laid hands on my mother, the same man who had threatened my family when I was only a boy. "I always wanted a chance to see that pretty little mama of yours just one more time. Too bad the bitch had to go and die before I found her again."

"Fuck you," I managed to get out. Everything was hazy, pain existed everywhere. I wanted to beat the hell out of this man, but I couldn't, I simply couldn't. My body refused to listen to what I told it and Searcher and Gunman weren't anywhere near through with me yet.

"Yeah? Well, we'll see who's fucked when all is said and done, Montana Thomas. I want you to take one thing with you to that Indian afterlife of yours. I might have been too late to take your mama, but that sister of yours? My, oh my, that is one fine piece of half-breed ass."

I tried to go after him, but my body pinned me to the ground. Searcher just laughed at my feeble attempts as big fat, lazy drops of rain landed on my face. Gunman let my head fall back to the ground, and I closed my eyes in defeat. I wanted to kill this man. I would have let the demons do what they would with me if I could have been granted just that one last request. Instead, I heard Gunman step back away from me.

"Make it slow," he told Searcher.

Searcher gave a satisfied laugh, and I heard him come closer.

"Wouldn't have it any other way," he said.

I'm not sure what he used, it wasn't his hands. After the first few blows, it didn't matter. The man knew his job; one must give credit where it is due. He stayed away from my head and face, knowing if he concentrated there, the pain would not be as effective. Instead he concentrated on my torso and already injured ribs, adding a few kicks to my arms and legs just for fun. Suddenly getting shot wasn't all that bad.

I tasted blood, but refused to give them what I thought they wanted, me begging for my life. It occurred to me that this attack on me was meant for my father's benefit. It had been two decades in the coming, but they were simply being thorough in following up on the threat they made to him then. They would kill his family, but let him live with the grief that he had caused their deaths. That would be his punishment for taking what was theirs.

I thought the first volley of gunfire was thunder. The rain had started to come down in earnest, the thunder and lightning occurring simultaneously. The storm had arrived, and we were in the dead center of it.

It took me a moment or two to realize that Searcher had stopped beating me. Maybe they thought I was dead. I remember being little and being so afraid of the thunder I would run to hide under the covers with my mother. I would curl up, afraid to move, frozen to her side.

"What's wrong, Montana?" she would ask me, ducking her head beneath the blankets.

"The sky monsters are looking for me, Mama," I would whisper to her.

"You're safe, silly boy. Your mama won't let any monsters get you."

I shook my head adamantly, I knew better. "If I move they'll find me, Mama. If I stay still they won't see me." As the storm subsided and the thunder diminished, I was certain that proved my point.

"See?" I would tell her. "They couldn't find me, I was very still and they went away."

As I lay there in the desert night, my blood mingling with the rain, I waited, careful not to move, for the thunder to fade and the monsters to go away. Somewhere in the back of my mind, I thought I heard my mother whisper to me. *"I'll take care of you. I won't let the monsters get you."*

I wanted to believe her.

CHAPTER 15

"Montana?"

The word was an intrusion I didn't want. I pushed it away. If I acknowledged it, I would have to acknowledge the pain that threatened to break through the blissful nothingness I had found.

"Open your eyes. Montana, come back, open your eyes."

"Don't want to!"

I was twelve and Dakota had found me. I had fallen off a bluff and broken my leg. By the time he found me I was feverish and beyond caring what happened to me. Luckily, Dakota was not.

He pushed and poked and basically bugged the hell out of me until I had no choice but to wake up just to tell him to stop. He stayed with me, got me to shelter and gave me water until Cal found us. One of the many times he saved me from myself.

"Montana."

I couldn't ignore the word. Reality pecked away at my quiet, painless existence and demanded to be recognized.

I opened my eyes and was greeted by my mother's face staring down at me. She was smiling and beautiful, just the way I remembered her. The image blurred and I blinked to bring it back into focus, then the pain found me.

"Make it go away, Mama. Make the monsters go away."

My mother continued to just smile back at me. I grimaced and shut my eyes again, hoping to find someplace to hide, someplace the pain couldn't find me.

"Montana?" The word was accompanied by a small slap to my face.

I tried to turn away from the simple assault, but wasn't allowed even that reprieve. My face was gripped, and when I opened my eyes again I found Dakota. I looked at him in confusion. Nothing made sense, then I tried to move my arm and the pain the movement caused me brought everything into alarming clarity.

A sound I didn't recognize escaped my lips, and I realized it came from me.

"It's all right, man," Dakota told me.

Is it? Doesn't feel all right.

"Dak?" I looked around and saw my mother again, still smiling at me.

Tate's cave. I'm in Tate's cave.

My mother's painted smile looked down on me. I think I smiled back, at least I did in my head, I'm not sure if it made it all the way to my lips.

I tried to move and felt every nerve in my body scream in protest.

"Just stay still," Dakota told me.

"Yeah, okay," I said. I was pretty sure I could do that.

"We need to get him out of here," I heard him say. I realized for the first time he wasn't alone. I tried to focus past him and saw David at his side, and Tate just behind him.

Everything came back to me then in a sudden dizzying rush. Gunman and Searcher, their promise to kill Tate and Dakota. They had no idea the danger they were in.

I bolted to a sitting position which was really only halfway to my elbow. The pain blossomed everywhere, angry and insistent. Everything danced around me, and the edges of reality blurred once more. I desperately tried to hold on to consciousness.

"David." I tried to get the words out before the darkness took me again. "They found you." I glanced at Tate and tried to swallow and tasted only blood. "*They know!*"

I coughed and my chest tensed with the pressure and pain. I remembered Searcher kicking me, the broken ribs. The concern I saw on Dakota's face made more sense to me now. If I looked only half as bad as I felt, he was probably terrified for me.

David edged in front of Dakota and pushed the hair away from my face. The gesture nearly broke me with its simple kindness.

"I know," he told me. "I know. We're safe. They're dead, we're all safe."

"They're dead?" I let him ease me back down, as if I had a choice.

"Yeah, they can't hurt you anymore." I thought I saw tears in his eyes, but maybe it was only a trick of the dim lighting in the small cave.

I wanted to believe him, it would be so easy to just believe him. I tried to make the pain back off a little. Maybe if I was very still it wouldn't be able to find me.

"See, Mama, told you."

"Look, he needs more than hope and a Band-Aid," I heard Dakota say to David. "He's in shock. Do you understand that? He will die if we don't get him to help and damn quick."

I heard Dakota's words and the urgency behind them, but couldn't work up the energy to get all that concerned over it. I could still hear him, but his voice started to fade and I let my eyes slide back to my mother's face painted on the wall above where I lay.

Outside, mixed with the pounding of the rain on the cave roof, I thought I could hear something else, something familiar. I smiled as I recognized the sound and looked at my mother.

"I hear them, Mama. I hear the coyotes."

She nodded at me, the painting suddenly come to life. It seemed perfectly logical to me.

"What are they saying to you, Montana?"

"They say they have come to take me home. I want to come home, Mama."

She shook her head and reached out a hand to touch my bruised and bloody face.

"Not yet, baby, not yet."

"I want to."

"You're too strong, you have too much living to do. I will wait for you but not yet."

She closed my eyes and Dakota's voice faded, and the pain went away for a little while. I never even thought to fight it, I looked for a way to follow my mother out of the dark, but she had left me there all alone. It was my last thought as I drifted away and gratefully embraced the numbness that had quietly wrapped around me.

Outside, the coyotes sang in the rain.

CHAPTER 16

There was a song I used to listen to in my teens. I couldn't remember the name of it or who sang it, but the lyrics kept repeating themselves in my head. *Out of time, out of space.* I could hear the music, but those few words were all I could I recall.

Out of time, out of space.

"What?"

"Out of time, out of space," I said, realizing I must have been sleeping, I opened my eyes to see who I was talking to.

"Dakota?" I asked. I blinked, looked again and then smiled, sure of it this time. "Dakota."

He smiled back, and his eyes filled suddenly as he gripped my hand tighter than I could take. I felt like a piece of paper, fragile and weightless. He readjusted his grip and I looked at him, confused, as tears fell down his face.

"Don't you ever do that to me again," he said.

"Okay, I won't. What exactly did I do?"

Dakota took a deep, shaky breath and scrubbed his face with the back of one hand. He sat down next me, and it was only then I realized I had no idea where I was. My last memory was being in Tate's cave listening to the coyotes. Looking around, I knew without a doubt this was not a cave. Fabric walls let soft, diffuse sunlight filter in. A tent, maybe?

"What do you remember?" Dakota asked me.

I thought about that and all I could get was the coyotes and those stupid song lyrics. I concentrated, and then gave him a head shake.

"Coyotes," I told him, knowing how that sounded. "I remember the coyotes. Where am I?" I asked trying to hitch myself up a little higher in the bed—not a bed, just blankets and furs piled on the ground. Dakota sat cross-legged next to me. When I couldn't accomplish the task, I looked down and discovered why. My left arm was tightly wrapped across my chest. Bandages around my torso and left shoulder left me completely immobile on that side. I didn't have the strength to compensate for the loss of one arm.

"It's a long story, you feel up to it?" he asked.

"Start talking."

Dakota smiled at the remark. "Okay, you're back," he said, nodding to himself as if he hadn't been sure of that fact up until now.

"Help me sit up first."

Dakota gripped my right wrist and started to help me sit, when the tent flap opened, spilling in brilliant sunlight and a cool breeze that chilled me, making gooseflesh bump up on my arm.

"Uh-oh," Dakota said, sounding much like a kid with his hand caught somewhere it shouldn't be.

I had enough momentum to hike myself up, and then Dakota propped me with a pillow. The tent flap closed again and I saw an old Indian dressed in a red checked flannel shirt, old Wrangler blue jeans and boots, with David directly behind him.

The old Indian starting rattling off in rapid Sioux to Dakota, who, to my surprise, answered him in passable if halting Sioux. I looked to David for some explanation, but he only smiled at me.

"What?" I finally asked. "Would someone mind filling me in?" I asked, starting to get a little annoyed.

The old Indian broke off his conversation with Dakota and centered his attention on me. He poked and prodded, and then he pointed to a small blossoming flower of red on the previously pristine white bandage. Every poke with his long, boney finger brought back a shadow of remembered pain. He let loose a string of expletives in Sioux, and he did not look happy.

I held up my hand and tried to stop him. I looked at Dakota, hoping for some mercy or at least pity.

"What is he so pissed off about?" I asked him, as the old man just kept rattling on regardless of the fact that I couldn't understand him.

"Well, technically, he's pissed at me," Dakota said. "I wasn't supposed to let you move until he saw you."

"And just who the hell is he? Ouch!" I yipped as the Indian probed tender ribs. I slapped his hand away and gave him a warning look. He gave me one back that made me regret doing so.

"He," David said, "is the shaman of his tribe, a much respected man. You owe him your life." David touched the old man on his shoulder and asked for his attention. When he had it, he made a little bow of respect.

"Chief Running Wolf, your grandson, Montana," David said.

My eyes went from the old Indian to David's in a flash. I started feeling a little lightheaded, as I looked to my father for an explanation.

The man waved away David's formal introduction. "Call me Walter," he told me, in perfect English. "My son has not been a visitor here for longer than I can remember, now he comes with three grandchildren I have never met before and one of them has nearly crossed over to the spirit world." He spared a glance for David. "He always was a nervy thing."

My father lowered his head, but I could see the smile spread across his face.

"Where's Tate?" I asked, noticing her absence for the first time.

"Sleeping," David told me. "Safe."

"What happened? Where is this place?" I needed answers to fill in the gaps in my memory, and no one was helping me out. "Please?" I was pleading and didn't care how it might sound.

David turned and spoke to his father in Sioux. Running Wolf—Walter—gave me a long look. "He has only just come back from the other side, make it brief," he told them and turned to leave.

"Chief." I realized I hadn't even thanked him. He opened the tent flap and turned his head in my direction. "Grandfather, thank you."

He inclined his head toward me and turned to Dakota. "Brief," he warned him.

"Another grandfather?" I asked after he had left.

"And a grandmother, not to mention an odd assortment of aunts, uncles and cousins," Dakota told me.

I slumped down into the covers again, feeling a little tired and a lot overwhelmed.

"Somebody start at the beginning," I begged.

David sat next to Dakota and began. "Not long after you took off, it started. It must have been your recent searches, or Tate's well-meaning but disastrous attempt at protecting me." He shrugged. "Doesn't matter, they finally found me. Always knew they would, just never thought it would happen the way it did." David closed his eyes and the recent past encroached. A past that nearly cost him the life of his children.

"I smelled the smoke and knew, I *knew!"* he said. "In that one instant I knew. They had set fire to the house.

"I sat in the kitchen, nursing a black eye and a bruised ego, and heard you drive away." David shook his head. "It was not the reunion I always envisioned. You were so angry, and I had nothing but the truth to give you. I always thought it would be enough. It wasn't."

I put a hand out to stop him. "Get to the point, David. The house was on fire?"

"I smelled the smoke first. When I opened the door to the living room, it was already fully engulfed. I knew you were out of danger, or so I thought, and I'd seen your brother walk down the drive earlier, but I had no idea where Tate was."

"Who, David? Who started the fire?" Nothing made sense, or maybe it did and I didn't want to accept it.

"They must have split up," Dakota said. "I was just past the bend in the drive, they didn't see me. But they saw what I missed—you leaving. They split up, two followed you and two stayed here. They set fire to the house knowing Tate was inside."

"You said she was okay," I said to David. He nodded and I saw fear in his eyes, fear from how close it must have come to not being okay.

"She is, thanks to Dakota."

I shifted my gaze to my brother who just shrugged.

"They planned on making me watch her die in the fire," David continued. "Dakota killed them."

"There was a rifle in the woodshed," he explained. "I could hear Tate screaming, I had to do something."

"And almost got yourself killed in the process," David said.

"What?" I tried to sound intimidating and pissed off as I looked at my brother. I'm pretty sure I didn't pull either one off.

Dakota simply feigned indifference and gave me a confused look. "I'm still here," he tried to argue.

"You stopped breathing," David reminded him.

I felt like I was watching a really bad tennis game and wasn't sure I had the energy to continue.

"So you jump-started me again and now we're even," Dakota told David.

"Could you cut to the chase, please?" I asked. I wasn't sure I could take any more revelations.

"We took a best guess as to where you went. Medicine Rocks seemed logical. Thank whoever was listening that your brother knows you as well as he does," David said. "We were almost too late as it was."

CHAPTER 17

I watched my father closely as he finished his story. I could see what it took for him to tell it, to relive it.

"We almost didn't get there in time," he said again, his voice choking with emotions. "I almost lost you all over again, boy."

I closed my eyes, partly to try to remember, partly because I was having difficulty keeping them open.

"I don't remember," I told him. It bothered me that I couldn't. The only thing that kept coming back to me was an image of my mother in the dark, telling me it wasn't time. *Time for what?*

Out of time, out of space.

God, I was losing it. "Dad, fill me in here. What happened, what is this place?"

David ran a hand over his hair and sighed. "I thought we were too late," he admitted. "When we got to you, I thought we were too late."

"We almost were," Dakota said.

"If we took you to a hospital, they would have found you. It wouldn't have been safe for you or the staff." David sighed. "I didn't know what to do."

I squeezed my eyes closed in attempt to remember something, anything, but I couldn't even recall driving out to Medicine Rocks.

Then there was something, a flash of memory. I glanced at my bandaged arm.

"They had a gun." It was really more of a question than a statement, but if the pain in my side and arm were any testament to what had happened to me, then I was pretty sure I had been shot.

David nodded, confirming what I had guessed. "I don't think they were aiming at your arm. They meant to kill you, Montana."

"Did you kill them?"

David nodded. "I'd do it again in a heartbeat." It was clear the topic was not a comfortable one. He changed subjects and spread his hands, indicating the tent we were in. "This is my father's home. Right now you have the privilege of being one of the few people alive to see it."

"Technically I haven't seen anything but the inside of a tent, yet," I told him.

"I drove us here from the desert, it took me awhile to remember the way, and then it took even longer to convince the scouts who I was."

"Scouts?" I asked.

"Running Wolf does not like visitors," David told me. "You had lost a lot of blood, broken ribs, God only knows what kind of internal injuries you might have had. There were times I didn't think you would come back to us, despite my father's care."

"Exactly how long have I been out of things?" I asked, confused.

Dakota looked at David and leaned forward, his arms resting on his bent knees. It appeared they'd been expecting the question and had decided Dakota should answer it.

"Four weeks, Montana. You have been in and out of it, delirious and fighting for every moment."

I had no response to that. *Four weeks, one month!*

"This is the first time you have been coherent since David brought you here." Dakota continued. "I'm almost afraid to let you go back to sleep."

I noticed how fatigued Dakota looked, the dark smudges under his eyes, the gauntness in his face. He didn't need to tell me he had not left my side for the entire time.

"I can't remember." It was all I could seem to say. The images were there right on the edge of my consciousness, but every time I tried to grab hold of them, they slipped out of my grasp once more, like trying to hold on to sand. Then I realized what David had lost. "Your home?" I asked, hoping against hope I was wrong.

He shook his head and waved my question away. "It doesn't matter, nothing matters except you're all right." He looked from me to Dakota. "All of you are all right and are here with me."

Glancing upward, I noticed the "tent" I was in was conical, very much like a tepee. "Exactly what is this place?" I asked.

The tent flap opened, and Walter poked his head through the slit. "This is not what I meant by brief, but I can see what I have been told is true. You are very much like my son—impatient."

The old man entered the tent fully and picked my right arm up and felt for a pulse. Looking down at his wrist I was a little surprised to see a watch there. The clash of technology and the time warp I seemed to have entered was a little unsettling.

"Too fast," he said, meaning my pulse. "He needs rest. A couple units of blood wouldn't kill him either, but you can't have everything you want."

I looked at Dakota, confused.

"You're not going to believe this," Dakota said. "But Walter here is a doctor, as in *M.D.* Graduated from Harvard."

"I think my grandson is a bit overwhelmed." Walter smiled at me, the look on my face must have been amusing. All I could figure out was I had been lying around in a tepee, being cared for by a grandfather I never knew I had, whose son was a father I had only just discovered, after nearly being killed by a couple of idiots with long memories and exquisite aim.

Everything started to spin, and I almost wished I was back in the dark. *Out of time, out of space.* I hurt, I could barely keep my eyes open, and I had no real idea of where I was. No one was answering my questions to my satisfaction, and I couldn't seem to figure out how to ask them any clearer. Everyone else was in on the joke and no one cared to share the punch line with me.

"You have a month of catching up to do," Walter told me. "Don't expect to get all the answers to all your questions at once. But I will tell you one thing. No one will find you here. You are safe for the moment. I have seen to that. You need to rest and heal, the answers will wait for you, so will we." My grandfather took my hand and held it to his chest. "Do you feel that? Do you feel the life there?"

I felt his heart beat slow and steady beneath my hand. I nodded to him.

"That is what you have been searching for, Montana. All your life you have looked for where you came from, never once stopping to consider why you needed to know."

It was as if this man I had just met looked directly into my soul and pulled it out to show it to me. The experience was at once enlightening and painful. My usual rock solid defenses were down; I couldn't even remember how to build them anymore, wasn't sure I wanted to. Somehow, looking into the man's dark eyes, it didn't seem that important.

"I will tell you a secret, boy." Walter leaned close. The whisper he spoke in was not meant for secrecy, it was clear he intended everyone in the room to share in his wisdom. "We are all connected, by blood or circumstance, it doesn't matter. What one man does, will in time, affect another. The things we do are ripples, stones thrown in the water, they grow and spread. Life is a circle, but the trick is we must stand within the circle to see it. You have been standing on the outside trying to fight your way in when all you had to do was turn around and look. The answers would have found you, Montana."

Walter put a gnarled, weathered hand out and cupped my face. The gesture was one of love and tenderness that I found almost painful in its honesty.

"You are young and impatient. You think you must always go and find those things that right now are so important to you. That is the way of youth." His eyes found his son's, and he smiled a sad smile. "They think their way is the only way, and no one can tell them differently."

I saw a tear escape my father's eye at the same time a small smile found his lips. It was clear at that moment what he had given up in order to stand outside his circle.

"What this old man is trying to say…" Walter turned his attention back to me and his hand moved to smooth hair off my face. "Is have patience with yourself. Your questions will all be answered, but not now."

His hand moved from my head to my face, closing my eyes, it stayed there as he spoke ensuring I would not open them again. I felt his skin on the palm of his hand, calloused and hard, but at the same time gentle and strong.

"Now, listen to this old man." This time he did whisper for my benefit only. "Sleep, heal, I will keep the demons at bay. They cannot find you here."

I believed him. I didn't think to ask how he knew about the things I feared in the dark. I took a deep breath, held it, and let it out slowly. I think sweet sleep found me before the breath had fully left me.

* * * *

I stood outside a circle drawn in the sand, looking in. I tried to cross over to gain entry, but was denied. Again and again I tried. I could walk around the circle, I could even walk away from it, but to enter it seemed beyond my power. It was as if an invisible barrier had been erected around the perimeter, denying me access. I couldn't figure it out. I looked closely, but all I could see was a line made in the earth. Like a child had drawn it on a whim, shaky and not entirely round. Just a simple circle, why the hell couldn't I step inside it?

"You're doing it all wrong, you know."

I looked up, surprised to see someone there. Someone from inside the circle talking to me. The light had dimmed and backlit the stranger, but his voice was familiar.

"What?" I asked, not completely understanding what he had meant.

"Well, I mean exactly what I said. You are doing it all wrong. You want in, right?"

"Yeah, why am I doing it wrong?"

The man standing inside the circle took a step toward me and laughed. "Ah, see, I'm not allowed to tell you. You have to figure that one out all on your own."

"So, you're allowed to tell me I'm doing it wrong, but you can't tell me why?"

"Pretty much."

I leaned forward, trying to see past the shadows to get a glimpse of the man's face, but whenever I moved, so did the light, denying me what I wanted.

"And exactly who told you that?" I wanted to know. "Who's making up the rules around here?" I walked the periphery of the circle and my "friend" followed me step for step, always just inside the shadows as he moved with me.

"Oh, come on, Montana, stop asking questions you already know the answers to."

Deciding I'd had about enough of all of this, I turned and walked away, trying to convince myself that entering the circle was not important to me at all. I took two, maybe three steps and found myself right back where I started, on the edge of the circle.

"Not that easy, my friend," the man inside the circle told me.

I turned again, determined to just walk away and again was denied, the edge of the circle at my feet once more. Frustrated, I took a step, but the circle held its boundaries.

"What the hell do you want from me?" I yelled. I couldn't go forward. I couldn't go back, and I could not figure out what I was supposed to do next. For once in my life I couldn't find the answers, I could not fix this. I fell to my knees in frustration. "Tell me!" I begged the man in the circle. "Tell me what am I supposed to do."

Squatting down, his arms resting on bent knees, the man brought himself to my level and shook his head. He looked liked a disappointed teacher, who, in trying all methods of instruction, simply could not get through to his student.

"You already know the answer to that," he said. The light suddenly shifted, and I could see the man's face for the first time. I sat back on my heels and stared.

My own face stared back at me from inside the circle.

"Sometimes the answer is so close, you have to take a step back to see it," I said to myself.

Then the me that was inside disappeared and when I looked to find him, I found myself, instead, standing in the exact center of the circle.

CHAPTER 18

I woke, covered with sweat, my heart hammering so loud in my chest, I was certain everyone nearby could hear it as well. I took a deep breath and then another, until the dream slipped away. The images in my head were confusing and left me feeling unsettled and jumpy.

Now very much awake, I sat up, pleased I could actually do so. My head was clear. A wave of dizziness was there and gone again in a moment. I was in the same tent, and it was night. Dakota slept on one side of me and our father on the other. I sat perfectly still and tried to figure out a way to get up without waking them. My head was too full of questions to deal with theirs.

I pushed the covers off and got to my knees as quietly as I could. My body told me in no uncertain terms that it had been ill-used and treated badly in the recent past. Ribs that had just begun to mend pulled against each other, reminding me I was very far from where I had been a few short weeks ago. I gritted my teeth and made a quiet groan as I got to my feet.

Giving a quick glance over my shoulder, I convinced myself that Dakota and David still slept, then silently pushed open the tent flap and breathed the fresh night air for the first in a very long time.

I just stood there, my eyes closed, head tilted back, and breathed. I felt worn out, used up and deflated, but I was alive, damn it, and I planned on staying that way. Taking a good look around was not easy.

The darkness was complete and denied me access. I saw other large tepees constructed throughout the trees. Small fires burned outside some of them. We were in the mountains, I didn't know that until just then. It was as remote a place as I have ever been in my life.

I heard water not far off in the distance and headed toward it and away from the little camp. The going was rough and hampered by my weakness. Taking baby steps and shuffling along feeling for hidden obstacles with my feet, I moved like I was a hundred years old.

My adventure was cut short when I tripped over a fallen log I failed to notice. Going down hard, I landed on my injured left side. With my arm still bound to my side, I had no way to prevent the fall and landed with an involuntary cry of pain. I rolled as the breath was crushed from my lungs and didn't think to object when hands came to my rescue and helped me sit up.

"Idiot, what do you think you're doing?"

As the stars dancing in front of my eyes faded and I was sure I could manage moving without further humiliation, I looked over to find Tate crouched down next to me.

"Apparently, falling down," I said, when I could, trying to hold on to the last ounce of dignity left to me.

Tate shook her head as she sat next to me. "God, save me from the men in my life. Are you all right?"

"Well, I'm not dead, so I guess that qualifies as all right." I tried for my best smile, but the look on her face told me she wasn't buying any of it.

"Don't," she said. I saw the tears then. I hadn't noticed them before, how could I have not seen them?

"Tate?" I asked, confused. She had gone from irritated to crying in a heartbeat, and I had no idea why.

"No," she said pulling herself together. "You're not dead, but God!

Montana, you have no idea how close you came. I do!"

"Okay, I'm sorry I almost died on you?" I asked, trying to find a way to appease her.

When she just shook her head and looked away, I had no idea what to say to her. That was a first, women were usually the part of my life I had no problems with. But then I remembered this woman was my sister, which brought an entirely new complication to the mix.

"So, how did you come to be my rescuer this evening—morning, I don't know which one it is," I admitted.

"Technically, I guess it's morning, a little after two." Pushing her hair away from her face with both hands, she crooked her knees up and hooked her arms around them. "I couldn't sleep, too quiet in this place and too many things going on up here." She tapped the side of her head and smiled. "I was sitting outside looking at the stars when I saw you leave. You didn't look too steady on your feet." She lifted her shoulders in a shrug. "Thought I better keep an eye on you."

Holding my left arm with my right, I tried to find a comfortable position. My hand came back red with blood. Tate watched me.

"The old man is gonna be pissed," she said and finally graced me with a real smile. "You sure you shouldn't go back and lie down?"

"That is all I've done for the last four weeks. I couldn't sleep, too much going on up here." I smiled and tapped the side of my head.

Tate sighed. "God, Montana, I thought you were dead. When I saw you there, all that blood, you weren't moving…" Her eyes had a haunted look as she seemed to relive the memory, no tears this time, just disbelief I think, at what had happened to her, to her life.

"I remember the cave," I told her. "I get nothing after that. Next thing I remember besides some weird dreams is waking up here."

Tate hugged her knees. "Be grateful for that small favor. It was raining, Dakota was freaking, the car was too far away to carry you, so we dragged you inside. At least it was out of the weather."

"You dragged me through that tunnel?"

She gave me a laugh. "Yeah, and let me tell you something, you are no lightweight, pal. Not that I'm complaining or anything, I am kind of fond of the way your particular parts are put together."

I couldn't help but smile at that.

"Montana?"

The look on her face said enough. I didn't know if I could go there just then. I wanted to put a halt to where the conversation was headed. "Tate, don't."

"Oh, so are we just supposed to ignore the eight-hundred-pound gorilla in the room?" she asked.

"David Willows, Jacob Willowcreek," I started.

She put her hands up and stopped me. "Yeah. I get it, Montana. We have the same father." She let out a breath and studied the night. "Never did have much luck with men. Not that there was a lot to choose from in Ekalaka. Anyone worth getting involved with never stayed. Then you come waltzing into my life. I mean, God, look at you! Testosterone has your picture next to it in the dictionary, my friend. And don't tell me you didn't feel it too, that spark from the very beginning, it was there." She turned her face toward me, daring me to deny it. I made the mistake of looking at her. Those eyes, so blue even in the dark, grabbed me and refused to relinquish the hold they always had on me.

"No," I said, "I won't deny that." What the hell, I decided, this was probably the only chance I would ever get to say the things I wanted to say to her. "I took one look at you, and I felt it. There you were, this bitchy, little thing full of 'I dare you to' attitude and I thought to myself, now *that* would be a challenge."

Tate smiled and looked away.

"I also thought I had never seen a more beautiful woman in my entire life."

Tate swung her head back to look at me, challenging me to tell her I was kidding. I wasn't.

She reached a hand out and touched me, my face. Her hand lightly traced the bruises still evident there, and then swept the hair off my face.

"You're the beautiful one, Montana Thomas, and I'm not just talking about the outside package." Her hand slid down to my chest, half covered with bandages. "You have a good heart. You're a sweet, decent man, Montana, no matter how hard you try not to let that part of you show to the world."

I took her hand from my chest and held it, mostly to keep her from touching me. "I'm not feeling very decent right now, Tate."

"Can you do something for me?" she asked.

Tilting my head I looked at her with suspicion. "Guess that depends on what that thing is."

Tate sighed. "I want to pretend for just one moment that we don't know what we know." She closed her eyes, looking like a little girl making up a story. "Let's pretend we just met and the rest of the world can't bother us. I'm the most beautiful woman you have ever seen and you? Well, you're you. Can we do that, Montana? Can we pretend?" She opened her eyes, asking me for just that one thing.

"Tate." I didn't know what to say to her.

She blinked and the tears that had been brimming, spilled down her cheeks again. "Don't say no, I'm not asking for something you can't give me, I'm not that desperate. I just want a kiss, just one kiss. No one has to know, no one but us. I just want to know what could have been. Is that so wrong? Am I such a horrible person for wanting that, for wanting you?"

Her honesty was disconcerting. God, I wanted that too, but I was afraid it wouldn't end with a kiss. My head kept telling me she was my father's daughter, but my heart refused to listen. I gave her one moment and I pretended.

"No, it doesn't make you horrible, it makes you human." I leaned toward her, hampered by my bandaged arm. It was not as graceful a move as I would have liked to make, but I managed. With her eyes still closed, I touched her face with my good hand and found the skin there was just as soft as I imagined it would be.

"Open your eyes, Tate. Look at me."

When she did, I wiped the tears from her cheeks with a finger, then cupped the back of her head with my hand.

"I wish it could have been different, I wish I could have been someone else for you," I said. "I wish I could give you more."

Brushing my lips against hers, I felt her tremble, and I pulled back to look at her. She turned and put her arms around my neck and closed the distance between us. She kissed me quickly, barely touching me and pulled away again. I shook my head at her hesitation.

"You put on this tough act, thinking you have to show that side to the world to protect yourself, don't you?" I said. "Tough little girl. You don't have to play that game with me, I know better. This is a one time deal, Tate, and that pitiful excuse for a kiss isn't what either of us wants."

I pulled her close, the fact that she didn't resist told me I had guessed right, she wanted the contact as much as I did, but she was scared. My lips touched hers and she leaned into me, holding me. Knowing this would not ever happen again, she poured everything into one kiss. It was one moment to last a lifetime.

I pulled back because I needed to, not because I wanted to. She opened her eyes and smiled at me.

"It would have been good, we would have been good together," she said.

I touched her face one last time and let my hand trail down her silky hair. "It's not a total loss, you know. You have no idea what it means to be part of this family. You just inherited two big brothers."

Tate sniffled and wiped her face. "Oh, don't I know it. I just spent four weeks worrying over one and dealing with the other. Dakota can be a bit annoying at times, did you know that?"

I laughed. "Yeah, I noticed. But if you need someone on your side, there is no one else I would want there."

"I know that too. He saved my life, remember?"

"Mine too, more times than I want to remember and in more ways than one." I looked out into the night and found a little comfort there. "Dakota is my best friend, I don't think I ever told him that."

"I wouldn't worry," Tate said, turning away and setting her gaze on the darkness with me, "I'm pretty sure he knows. I have a feeling he feels the same way about you. He's barely left your side the entire time."

An image of Dakota's tired face came into my head. "I could tell. He looks exhausted."

"I offered to sit with you, to give him a break, let him get some sleep." She shook her head. "He refused. He is almost as stubborn as you." She turned her head, and I felt her scrutinize me. Things had returned to normal between us, we had our moment and it was over.

"He's worse," I told her, and smiled.

She turned back to the darkness surrounding us, and silence wrapped softly around us once more. The strength that greeted me on waking had long vanished. I felt the need to go back and sleep, but wasn't sure I had the energy to accomplish the relatively simple task. It was frustrating and humiliating to admit. I wasn't used to being the needy one.

The last time I could remember feeling anywhere near this helpless was in the army when I nearly had my leg blown off. Even the months in rehab I felt strong, but then I had been fortunate to sleep the worst of it off in drug-induced bliss in an ICU. I didn't have that luxury here. Somehow I didn't think the worst was done with me yet.

Right now, sitting up seemed to take all my combined strength and energy.

"Hey, Montana?" Tate's quiet voice pulled me out of my self-pity.

"Yeah?"

"Promise you won't let anyone in on my secret?" she asked.

"Secret?" We had shared many in the last few minutes, and I wasn't sure which one she meant.

"That I'm not all that tough?"

I laughed just a little. "No problem, I'll keep yours if you keep mine."

She grinned, but cocked her head at me, confused. "What's yours?"

"I don't think I can get up," I said in all honesty.

The thought of walking all the way back to the tent seemed too daunting a task to even consider. I could feel blood, warm and sticky against the cool night air, trickling down the inside of the bandages on my arm. My legs felt like they were made of clay, and my head buzzed. I wasn't worried, I thought I'd just pushed myself too hard, I probably should have stayed in bed. But if I had done that I would have missed Tate. To me, whatever happened next was worth it for that one small favor the fates decided to grace me with.

The look of confusion on her face turned to one of concern in an instant. I felt sorry I'd been the one to put it there.

"Oh my God, Montana. Do you want me to get Dakota?"

"No!" I said louder than I intended. "No. Hell, he turns into a mother hen when he thinks someone is hurt."

"You are hurt," Tate reminded me.

"Exactly, he'll never let me forget it. Please, I was kind of hoping you could help me." I beseeched her with my eyes.

"Just me? Umm, don't know how to tell you this, pal, but you outweigh me by like a hundred pounds." She raised her brows at me.

"I didn't say you had to carry me, just help me to my feet, I think I can make it from there." I wasn't at all sure of that, but I was desperately trying to hold on to whatever dignity I had left to me in her eyes.

Tate got up and stood in front of me. "You sure? I don't want to hurt you. I don't know what to do."

I held out my right arm and reached for her forearm. She grabbed me and pulled. Despite the pain, it should have worked, but I wasn't counting on the spasm that gripped my ribs and cut off my air, or the knife-edged pain that ripped through me when I tried to stand. The grass made slick by the night dew denied me purchase and caused my feet to slip. I fell hard on my back and inadvertently pulled Tate down on top of me. All one hundred and ten pounds landing directly on freshly broken bones.

If it didn't hurt so freaking bad, I probably would have laughed. As it was, I couldn't even catch my breath. There was no way she could crawl off me without hurting me more. A knee in a mending rib, her hand gripping the wound on my arm, fresh jabs of agony flared to life and squeezed the air from my lungs.

"Oh God! Montana!" She jumped off me. "Are you all right? Idiot, of course you're not all right. Oh God, I told you I couldn't do it! Why did you ask me?"

"Tate," I said as loud as I could, but it came out as a whisper, my breath refusing to cooperate.

"I'm sorry," she said, not hearing me.

"Tate!" I said again, louder this time.

Finally getting through to her, she stopped moving around in a blind panic and looked at me. I was very much aware of how I must have looked to her, curled up in a fetal ball, my face pinched with pain but trying not to show it. Pretty much pathetic. I had no pride left at the moment. Funny how pain can do that to you.

I made sure I had her attention before I spoke, not wanting to waste precious breath. "Tate?"

"Yeah?" she asked, close to tears again, but at least she stilled and listened to me.

"Now you can go get Dakota."

She paused for a moment as the words sunk in. "Oh, yeah, right," she said and took off at a run.

I knew I would pay dearly and probably for the rest of my life for admitting I needed Dakota, but I would deal with that later. Life had a way of evening the score. You never knew what it was going to throw at you, all you could do was go with whatever came your way.

CHAPTER 19

I tried to get up. I hoped by the time Tate got Dakota I would be on my feet and halfway back to the tent. Didn't quite work out that way. That old cliché about being beaten within an inch of your life suddenly became excruciatingly clear to me. I had a feeling that was what had happened to me. Five minutes more, give or take, and Gunman and Searcher would have completed their task, so I supposed I should've felt grateful for the pain, it meant I had survived. I was having a little difficulty working up the gratitude though, when the simple task of breathing brought tears to my eyes.

I lay exactly how Tate had left me, curled in a ball, shivering, miserable and pissed. When I got it back together again, someone was going to pay for putting me at Dakota's mercy. I gritted my teeth as I heard them coming.

"He's here!" I heard Tate say.

A moment later Dakota was kneeling next to me. I saw the look of panic on his face and guess I deserved it, but I tried to diffuse him anyway.

"Chill, man, I'm okay. Just need a hand getting up." I tried to make my voice sound relaxed and calm, but even I could hear the weakness in my words. I shook with a deep internal chill that had nothing to do with the night air.

"Jesus, Montana! What are you trying to do, finish what they started?"

"Dak." I didn't know what I intended to say, Dakota never gave me the chance to find out.

"Shut up," he yelled at me.

I must have been pretty bad if I had no reply for that.

"He ripped open the sutures, that much is for sure," another voice said off to my side.

I followed the voice with my eyes, the only part of me that didn't hurt and wasn't overly surprised to find David there.

He turned his head and spoke to Tate. "Go wake the old man. Tell him what happened, tell him to meet us back at the tent, and Tate?" I watched Tate tear her eyes from me and look back at her father. "Tell him to hurry."

That unglued her feet and she tore off into the trees.

"Don't you think you're being a little dramatic there, Dave?" I asked. My voice was quiet, but at least it had stopped shaking.

My father knelt on the other side of me, his hands moving over me. I thought it was odd I couldn't feel his touch, but didn't think to ask anyone about it. I was so cold, but the pain made it through despite that. At my question, he stopped and turned my face toward his own. His touch was gentle, and I couldn't be sure but I thought I felt his hand shake, or maybe it was me.

"Montana, you should never have been out of bed. Listen to me. The men who are after me, the ones who did this to you? They weren't amateurs, do you understand? Besides the bullet wound in your shoulder, they broke nearly every rib, hard to tell without x-rays, but we didn't have that luxury. My father is fairly certain your spleen took a pretty good hit. Think back to basic anatomy. You rupture your spleen, you die without surgery. You've lost a lot of blood internally.

We've been holding our collective breath for four weeks and just when it looked like you might actually be turning the corner, you go and do this!" David put a hand to my head and lowered his in frustration, or disbelief. "Damn it, Montana." He looked over to Dakota. "He's hot. We need to get him back to the tent."

"And exactly how are we supposed to do that without killing him in the process?" he asked.

"We carry him," he said.

It was almost funny. They were discussing me, but I felt very far removed from the conversation. A stranger in my life.

The tent was maybe a one-minute walk from where I lay, but the jostling and sheer pain of being lifted and carried by David and Dakota made it feel like a lot longer. At one point I wished I would just black out and let them do what they had to, but someone was majorly pissed at me—I stayed conscious and remembered everything.

Tate and my grandfather were already waiting for us when they finally laid me down again. Dakota immediately was all over me. I wore no shirt, but he took a pair of scissors provided by Walter and proceeded to cut away the bloodied, filthy bandages across my chest and arm.

I needed a minute to catch my breath, just a minute. "Wait." I put a hand up to stop him, and it was pinned down against my side. It didn't occur to me to object.

"Dakota?" I asked, grimacing as he pulled the bandage off.

He answered with a quick flick of his eyes to mine, but didn't stop what he was doing. "Yeah?"

"I'm going to remember this," I warned him.

That got a smile out of him. "God, I hope so."

"Count on it," I said, but I don't think he heard me.

Walter and David brought several lanterns and placed them around me, and then my grandfather took over. His hands were gentle, but he couldn't help the pain they caused.

Wiping the blood from my arm, he nodded in agreement with David's assessment. "Well, he was thorough, I give him credit for that. Ripped every one of my sutures out. Actually it's just as well."

His fingers pressed on the open, swollen wound, eliciting a cry of pain from me. I looked at what he was doing and saw a stream of thick yellow fluid flowing from the wound. It hurt like a bitch.

"It's infected. Probably why he has a fever." He shoved a thermometer under my tongue. "Keep it there," he warned me and moved his hands to my side and chest, and then more gently to my abdomen. "Take a deep breath."

I tried but I couldn't quite do it, hurt too damn bad. Bringing my legs up to ease the pain, my grandfather removed his hands and took the thermometer from my mouth.

"His spleen is still enlarged and tender, but I don't think he did any additional damage. The problem now is he's septic."

"What's that mean?" Tate asked.

Dakota took the thermometer from Walter and looked disgusted as he read it. I couldn't figure out what he was so pissed at.

"A hundred and three." Turning to Tate, he explained, "It means the wound is infected to the point where his system can no longer fight back. He needs to be in a hospital," he said in frustration.

"And if we take him to one, the people who sent the men who hurt him, will find him and us, and they'll finish what they started," David said.

"So, you're telling me he's dead either way?" Dakota asked. "No. No way, I refuse to believe that. Montana is not going to die, I won't allow it."

"Dakota," I said, waiting for his attention. "I'm not going to die." The thought seemed absurd to me.

"Dakota." Walter turned his attention to my brother, his voice one of quiet authority. Calm in the center of the storm. "There is always more than one way. I know it is not what you've been taught, it's not what I was taught, but modern medicine is not always the best choice."

"No offense, Grandfather, but he's septic, you tell me how else to fix that without antibiotics and IV fluids." Dakota was at the end of his patience, I could tell by the tone of his voice. I needed to talk him down, convince him that it was going to be all right, Walter did it for me.

He stood and walked around me to where Dakota waited on the other side. He took my brother's face in both aged hands and smiled. "Have some faith in the old ways, Dakota. I have no intention of letting this grandson I have only just met die on me. He has been an incredible pain in the ass, and I intend to make him pay for every sleepless night he has caused me over the last month. But I find myself in need of assistance. Could you find a kettle of hot water and bring it to me? I should think your grandmother would have one on the fire outside our tent."

"You're trying to get rid of me," Dakota surmised, but his voice was calmer and he seemed more in control than he had been moments earlier.

"Yes, I am, but it doesn't mean I don't need the water."

Dakota, recognizing defeat, or perhaps knowing he had met his match, did as he was asked.

"I'll be back," he said to me, then turned to fetch his water.

"He's just worried," I said. "He doesn't like things being out of his control."

"He comes by that honestly. Neither do I." Walter turned back to me. He took his time, knelt down and touched my head, the way a parent comforts a sick child. I guess in a way, that is exactly what he was doing. "Montana, I won't lie to you, I'm not sure I can fix this. Do you understand what I am telling you?"

"That I could die." I never considered that a possibility until that moment. I couldn't die, I was only twenty-nine. I tried not to show the fear that made a sudden appearance in my soul.

My grandfather gave me a nod. "I will do what I can so that does not happen. I meant what I told your brother, I intend to make you pay for my many sleepless nights." He smiled at me. "Now I will tell you something else. The infection in your arm needs to be excised. I need to cut the wound open to let the sickness there drain, and I can give you nothing for the pain. With the condition you are in, that alone could kill you. I'm sorry."

I felt something being wrapped around my wrists and looked to see David restraining my arms with strips of cloth.

I shook my head, understanding they meant to tie me down to do what they had to so. "No," I said. The thought of being helpless scared me more than the pain my grandfather promised me. I pulled my right arm back before it could be restrained. "No!" I said, louder, the fear and anger coming through in the one word.

"You won't hold still, Montana, no matter how hard you try. No one is that strong," my grandfather told me.

I closed my eyes and felt unwanted tears course hot and wet down my face, I let my father tie me down, so my grandfather could put a knife to me. I tried to put myself someplace else, anyplace but here.

"I'm here, man, right here." I heard Dakota's voice and opened my eyes to see him seated at my head, his hands resting on my shoulders.

I felt a shiver go through me as the tent flap opened and another man entered. I didn't know him, but assumed he was another of

Walter's *family*. He positioned himself at my feet, his hands resting on my ankles. As I looked down the length of my body it was unrecognizable to me, covered in a myriad of bruises and cuts, the muscles I worked so hard to maintain wasted and weakened by a month of inactivity. I was not the same man I had been the last time I had seen myself.

"Montana." My grandfather spoke my name softly. I looked over at him. "We're ready."

I met his eyes and tried to be brave, I was always the brave one, but I wasn't sure I could pull it off this time. Maybe they should let me die, did I have that choice? The restraints cinched tight around my extremities, and I tried to prepare myself. Dakota leaned his weight onto my shoulders as the man at my feet grabbed my ankles and did the same. I noticed Tate in the room for the first time as she took up a position at my right arm with David at my injured left side.

Walter ran a surgical blade over a flame, then poured alcohol on it. I watched hypnotized by the silent procedure, then I turned my head away. I didn't want to look and couldn't work up the energy needed to care if that made me seem like a coward. I closed my eyes and waited for my grandfather to put the knife to my arm.

I tried to keep it under control. The blade bit into flesh quickly and precisely, and the pain set my entire world on fire. My grandfather was right, even with restraints and four people holding me down, I bucked and pulled against the hell unleashed inside of me. Even as a child, I can't remember screaming in pain the way I did then. It was beyond my control. I wanted out, I prayed to whoever might be listening to make it stop. *God, please just make it go away!* I looked for the darkness, but that peace was far away and not listening to my pleas.

Then it was done. Collapsing against the hands that held me, I cried quietly as the pain was not through with me yet. My grandfather squeezed the newly opened wound, and I found the courage to look at the offending limb. It was difficult to believe this bloodied, putrid mess was a part of me. Thick yellow-green pus rolled from the open wound, mixed with blood, lots of blood.

When my grandfather was satisfied he had tortured me sufficiently, he turned to Dakota. "That is all I can do for now. Dress the wound, lightly, let it drain. Clean him up, a bath might help get his temperature down."

If Dakota made a reply, I didn't hear it, my attention was riveted on my grandfather. At that moment, in my delirium and agony, I hated him. If I could have, I would have killed him, without a doubt in my scrambled brain.

My grandfather seemed to understand and actually smiled at me. "I am sorry, grandson," he said, and I heard emotions thick and just barely contained. He leaned over my battered, bloodied body, pushed my hair from my face and kissed my head.

I had no words for that. None. I simply stared at the man. He gave a nod to David and left the tent.

My arm throbbed and burned. I shivered and thought of all the times I had been told to go to hell. I was there, and it was not fun.

Dakota took the water he had brought and without a word, started to bathe me. Tate and David helped him. This time the hands that touched me were gentle, almost in apology for the assault moments earlier. I closed my eyes and let them do what they would. I had no fight left in me. I didn't care.

The darkness finally took pity and claimed me for its own. I embraced it gratefully and slipped quietly into a place where the pain could not follow me.

Chapter 20

"Do you believe in God, Dakota?" I don't remember how old we were, young, maybe nine and ten.

He was watching a movie and shrugged. "I don't know, why?"

"Well, I was just thinking, you know."

"Yeah? Don't hurt yourself." He laughed at his own joke. His sense of humor developed at an irritatingly early age.

Ignoring him, I continued with my train of thought, I was really talking to myself anyway. "You know how mom is always telling us about the spirit world and how the Great Spirit watches over all of us? And then I read about God and Jesus and heaven?"

"Yeah?" Dakota turned to look at me. "What about it?"

"Well, I was just wondering which was true, does it matter? I mean, if you believe in the Great Spirit and he doesn't exist will God be mad at you? Or will the Great Spirit send you away if the opposite is true?"

Dakota shrugged, his attention on me now instead of the movie. "Never thought about it."

"Just being stupid, I guess," I said, trying to make it not sound as important as it felt at the time.

"No, I mean I think it's important to think about this stuff from time to time," Dakota said, and seriously considered the question. "I'll tell you what I think."

I leaned forward, interested in what he might have to say on the subject.

"I don't think it matters what you believe in. I don't think any higher power worth believing in would get mad at you for just trying to figure things out—you know? I think people get too wrapped up in names and forget that we are all in this together. Deep down we all believe the same thing."

"We do?" I asked him.

"Yeah, you know that there is something up there, out there that cares about us, that cares whether we live or die, something that understands the things we run from, the things that scare us. They are the one we talk to when there is no one else to ask, when there is no one else to blame. It would be a crappy job—I wouldn't want it."

My brother, the philosopher at nine. He told me one of the most meaningful things I have ever learned in my life to date. I think he farted at that eloquent moment and went back to his movie.

It was a conversation I have returned to many times in my life. One that kept replaying over and over in my head as my own mortality hit me square in the face.

I felt as if my entire life was a flashback scene in a movie. Conversations I had as a kid, things I wish I would have said as an adult, played itself out in my dreams, or my subconscious. I couldn't tell where the dreams left off and reality sneaked in.

Where do you think you go when you die?

I heard Dakota laugh and opened my eyes.

"I don't know, but I'm glad you didn't find out just yet," he said.

"What?" I didn't realize the thought had made it out of my mouth. I blinked, trying to clear my vision and scrubbed a hand over my face, several days' worth of stubble greeted me there. I tried to shake the last vestiges of the dream. "Never mind." My last memories suddenly came to mind and I glanced at my arm. The bandage there was clean and dry.

"How you feeling?" Dakota asked me. He had been sleeping next to me, and I had woken him.

"Not sure, you tell me."

Dakota leaned up on his elbow and wiped sleep from his eyes with the heel of one hand. "Been a rough couple of days, man," he told me.

"For you or me?"

"Both, I think," he said.

"Tell me about it."

"Do you remember any of it?" he asked me.

"Most of it, unfortunately. I think I need to kick your ass for something. Remind me of that later, will you?"

"Happy to oblige." He grinned at me.

"So, I'm not going to die?"

"You tried hard enough, but, no, doesn't look that way."

I closed my eyes and took silent inventory. My head was clearer than it had been last time I was awake. Lying there quiet and still, I couldn't pinpoint any particularly painful parts. Somehow, I knew that would change the moment I decided to move. For the immediate future, staying where I was seemed like a good idea.

"Your fever broke last night. You've been sleeping ever since," Dakota told me.

I noticed the dim light coming through the tent and couldn't be certain if it was dawn or dusk.

"Day or night?" I asked Dakota.

He glanced at his watch, sat up and stretched. "Day, five-thirty in the morning to be exact. Can I trust you to stay put if I go get Grandfather?"

"Dak, I couldn't go anywhere if you stripped me naked and set fire to the tent."

"Well, I got the naked part covered." Dakota grinned.

I peeked under the blankets covering me and saw that he was right about that. I had vague memories of someone cutting my clothes off. "Yeah, what is it with that anyway? Can I have my clothes back now?"

"Technically, you don't have any clothes, the ones you were wearing are toast, but I'm sure we can find something for you. What else do you remember?" he asked with a wicked smile on his face.

"If what you're trying to find out is do I remember the gang-bath from hell, the answer is yes, you sick bastard. You do realize that Tate is our sister?"

"You know, that fact didn't seem to bother her too much." Dakota lifted the tent flap and started to leave when I called to him.

"Dakota?"

He turned around and raised his brows in a question. "Yeah?"

"I *am* going to get better eventually. I'm going to get my strength back, and then I am going to make you pay for this."

Dakota came all the way back into the tent and knelt next to me. "Montana, I just spent the last month trying to keep you alive and the last three days convinced I was going to have to go through another funeral, that I would be scattering your ashes in the Black Hills with Mom's. You slipped further and further out of reach and I thought 'hell I'm watching my brother die right in front of my eyes'. I've never felt so completely helpless, so if beating my ass for letting Tate see you naked is incentive enough to get you back on your feet, then listen carefully to this." Dakota leaned closer and grinned at me. "She washed all the good parts." He stepped back quickly and left me to think about that. I could hear him laughing all the way to get our grandfather.

Someone was going to pay for putting me at Dakota's mercy.

* * * *

My grandfather entered the tent a few minutes later with Dakota just behind him. He said nothing, or in no way acknowledged me. He simply knelt next to me and let his hands tell him what he needed to know. He touched my head with the back of his hand, then moved down my body. His hands were gentle and less demanding than I remembered them. Finally, he went to my left arm. I grimaced on the inside, but swore I would redeem myself and keep my face stoic. As he unwrapped the fresh bandage down to the skin, I wasn't prepared for what I saw. My last memories were colored in fever-induced delirium and couldn't be trusted.

The outside of my left arm, from the top of my shoulder to maybe the three inches above my elbow, was flayed open. Bloody gauze filled the wound which was a good half-inch across in places. The edges of the skin were red and touchy, but not nearly as painful as I remembered.

My grandfather looked at the wound he had inflicted, gave a grunt and nodded at my brother.

"It is better," he told Dakota. "Keep doing the dressing changes twice a day. I'll make sure you have the supplies you need."

Dakota nodded and took my grandfather's place as the old man stood. As my brother replaced the dressing, my grandfather acknowledged me for the first time.

"Have you decided to stay on this side of mortality for a while longer, young Montana?"

"For a while at the very least, Grandfather," I told him.

"Good, because you have been a burden around here for far too long. There are rules here, and I fully expect them to be followed, is that understood?"

"Yes, sir." I grinned and inclined my head toward him.

"You have today to rest, tomorrow you start earning your keep." My grandfather looked at Dakota, and they smiled at one another as if they shared a secret I was not supposed to be privy to. Reaching for the tent flap, he looked over his shoulder at me. "Montana, I am very glad the spirits were not quite ready for you to join them." Then he turned and left me alone once more with Dakota.

"Something you want to let me in on?" I asked him.

"Not particularly," he said. Then settling back down inside the blankets and furs that served as a bed, he turned his back to me. "Get some sleep, Montana. I have a feeling you're going to need it."

"Wait a minute, that's it? Gee, glad you didn't die, now get your ass in gear, we have work to do?" I didn't really mean it, but it was a ritual of sorts between us. The worse things were, the more we needed to make light of it. The more caustic the remarks, the better we were doing. It was sick and warped, but it worked for us.

"Shh, trying to sleep here," Dakota mumbled.

"Yeah, you sleep, I'm just lying here suffering, but don't worry about it."

"You want to talk about suffering? You try living with Grandpa Walt and the whole fricking posse for the last month. You spent most of that time oblivious to the fact that there is no running water, no indoor plumbing, and worst of all, *no coffee*!" Dakota kept his back to me and punched his pillow, then lay back down again. "Hell, the man gets the shit kicked out of him, gets shot and nearly bleeds to death, and he thinks he knows what suffering is!" he added.

"God," I said. "No coffee? I had no idea. You're right, you win. I apologize, you have been through sheer hell." I tried to keep the smile off my face, but as he wasn't looking at me, I figured it didn't matter.

I felt the weight of the last few days slide off me with the exchange. If Dakota could gripe to me about the interruption of his caffeine habit, I knew it was going to be okay. Judging by how weak I felt, I had no doubt that my recovery would be by no means a quick one. But I also knew there would be a recovery. I had doubted that fact for a short time.

"Montana?"

"Yes, Dakota?"

"Shut up and get some sleep."

I closed my eyes and had no problem doing just that. God, it was good to be back.

CHAPTER 21

Apparently my grandfather didn't believe in coddling the weak or injured. Early the next morning he flung open the tent flap, letting in the cool breeze. He threw me a bundle wrapped in a blanket and handed Dakota a small jar. "Put that on the wound, it will help draw the infection out like I told you, then wrap it like you have been," he told Dakota.

Dakota opened the jar and smelled it, then pulled it away, his expression making it very clear what he thought of the odor.

My grandfather turned his attention to me and the package I held. "Your grandmother made them for you. It would make her smile to see you wear them."

I unwrapped the blanket with one hand and saw a beautiful pair of handsewn buckskin pants and a matching shirt. They felt like velvet to the touch and had a short fringe running up the outside seam. They were almost white in color. The shirt was long-sleeved with fringes on the outside of the arm and matched the pants perfectly. A deep V held together with leather ties made it possible to pull the shirt over my head despite my injured arm.

"It's beautiful," I said, truly touched. "Tell her thank you."

"Tell her yourself. You need to get up today. Dakota knows the way." He gave Dakota a nod and left without another word.

"Why do I get the feeling that you two have some hidden agenda?"

"Got me." Dakota shrugged and started to take down the dressing on my arm. I winced as he pulled the old soiled gauze out of the wound. Then putting on a pair of latex gloves, he scooped up some of the salve Grandfather had given him.

I grabbed his wrist before he could touch me. "I don't think so," I told him as the smell hit me.

"Fine, I'll just go tell the old man you refuse to let me do this."

That was one complication I didn't consider. I might not admit it to anyone but myself, but my grandfather intimidated the hell out of me. I looked at the slightly yellow goo in Dakota's hand. "What is that anyway?"

"He told me it's made from several plants in the area. It has antibiotic properties and a mild anesthetic to help with the pain."

The no pain part was appealing, but the *smell*!

"Montana, the man saved your life, do you really think he would do anything to compromise that?"

I let out a frustrated breath, dropped the hand holding Dakota's wrist and let him smear the stuff into the wound. It was cold, but I wasn't prepared for the anesthetic to kick in on contact. The moment the goo touched the wound the nagging ache that had been there for days disappeared. I had no idea how much it hurt until the pain was gone. Muscles that I didn't realize were bunched and tense, relaxed. I let out a breath of relief and looked at Dakota in amazement.

"Damn, I have to find out what that stuff is made from."

"Well, I could tell you, but then I'd have to kill you. I have been sworn to secrecy." He grinned and raised his brows at me. "Better?"

"Yeah, hell yeah," I said and experimentally flexed my arm. The pain might have been diminished, but I was shocked at how weak I still was.

Motioning to the clothes I still held in my hand, Dakota asked, "Can you manage, or do you want some help?"

"I haven't needed help dressing since I was two. I think I'll manage. Hey."

"Yeah?"

"Is there anything resembling breakfast out there? I just realized I'm starving."

Dakota laughed. "I think that can be arranged. Get dressed, I'll be outside if you change your mind about the help, or you know, I could always go get Tate."

I threw the clothes at Dakota. He caught them easily and threw them back at me.

"I hate you," I told him, but couldn't keep the smile from my face.

I got up and dressed slowly, my movements methodical and stiff. I felt like a very old man. It was also the first chance I had to check out the damage done to me.

Yellow-brown bruises covered my chest, mostly on the left side. My hip on that side also sported an impressive yellow mark. I vaguely remembered Searcher making contact there with his boot. There was also a healing, but jagged slash on my neck just behind my right ear, reaching down to my collarbone. I had no memory of how I came across that souvenir. I wanted a mirror to see how bad my face looked, but there wasn't one. Using my hands to explore, I discovered raised skin above one eyebrow where stitches had been and scabs along my hairline. My nose felt whole, didn't think it had been broken.

I sighed and bent to pull the soft leather up over my hips. I had lost a lot of weight in the last four weeks. My hip bones jutted out and there was very little muscle definition left to speak of. For the first time in our lives, Dakota outweighed me. I pulled the drawstring tight, and vowed it was a condition that would not last long enough to matter. Carefully slipping the shirt over my head and placing my injured arm through the sleeve, I let my breath out slowly. The simple task of getting dressed had worn me out, but I was not about to give into it. I tried in vain to smooth my hair, but it was in desperate need of both a wash and a trim. I settled for pushing it off my face, then opened the tent flap and got my first good look at my new home.

Dakota had not gone far, waiting for me just outside. I squinted at the rising sun, wishing for my sunglasses as I tried to ignore my brother. He stepped back and appraised me, making me uncomfortable under his scrutiny.

"What?" I asked, looking down at myself.

"Nothing. Well, hell you look like something out of an old western. You know, I could get a black mask and be the Lone Ranger to your Tonto, what do you think?"

"I think I might have to hurt you."

"Yeah, but you'd have to catch me first."

"I'm remembering all of this, Dakota," I warned him.

Dakota came up beside me and put a gentle arm around my shoulders. "I missed you, Montana, don't do this to me again."

"Not if I can help it." I let him lead me, and I looked around. "Dakota, exactly where the hell are we?"

"Oh, yeah, I forgot you don't know. We were kind of at a loss as where to take you that night. I wanted to call nine-one-one and have you airlifted to the nearest trauma center. But David was certain that the guys who did this to you, the ones we killed, were only hired muscle. The guys who call the shots are still out there looking and once they realized that their hit men were dead, the first place they would look would be hospitals. We loaded you up and David drove us here."

"And where is here?" I asked again.

"The mountains, somewhere in the state of Montana, other than that I have no clear idea. David wouldn't tell me, and I wasn't paying attention during the drive. I was a little preoccupied trying to keep you alive. Apparently, Walter and David haven't spoken to each other in years."

"That sounds familiar," I admitted.

"Yeah, must be a genetic thing." He smiled. "Anyway, seems old Running Wolf was already a shaman, a respected medicine man, when he went to school for his MD. Now he uses a combination of the two practices and runs a free traveling clinic. He goes to all the reservations in the state, does what he can for free."

Dakota stopped about ten yards away from one of the tents, our destination I presumed.

"He is an amazing man, Montana. David told me he was disgusted with how his people were treated, how they treated themselves. He thought there had to be a better way. He took his family and anyone else who wanted to follow and came here. They live pretty much like they did a hundred years ago. A couple of times a month, when he's traveling with the clinic, he gets supplies, and then they come here each year to winter. No one knows about this place, no one bothers them. I've never seen anything like it. Except for the lack of coffee, it's incredible. They get and boil their own water and kill their food, supplemented by what he gets in town." He motioned to my clothes. "They even make their clothes from cured animal hides. Talk about a freaking time warp. I feel like I've been thrown back to the seventeen hundreds. Oh, by the way, Santee will not speak English. She understands it just fine, but refuses to utter one word, she insists the culture is being lost and we need to reclaim our heritage."

"Santee?" I asked.

"Our grandmother, David's mother. I have no words, she is something to be experienced not explained. You ready?" he asked.

"No," I said, a little unnerved.

"And you never will be." Dakota laughed. "Come on, big brother, I won't let her hurt you."

We walked the few feet to the tent and Dakota held the flap open for me. I entered, not quite sure what to expect. Sitting on the floor, braiding a young girl's hair, was an impossibly tiny woman, somewhere between sixty and seventy, it was difficult to tell. Her dark hair, streaked with silver, was tied at the nape of her neck and lay down her back in a thick rope. Her black eyes turned up to me as I entered. She finished the braid and whispered to the child, who skirted past me to leave.

"Santee," Dakota said from behind me. "Your grandson, Montana."

Santee got to her feet. Her head came to just about the height of my elbow. She walked around me, eyeing me critically, came around to face me once more, and started talking in rapid Sioux. She tugged on the hem of the shirt I wore and smoothed the fabric. I assumed she was asking me about the fit.

"It's very nice," I told her. "Thank you. It fits well."

She said something to Dakota who translated for me. "She says you need to eat, you're too skinny, but it fits you well enough. She also says you look like her son."

Santee sat back down and patted the ground next to her while looking at us. No translation was needed.

"Since when are you fluent in Sioux?" I asked Dakota, moving to sit next to my grandmother.

"After a month of listening to nothing else, it kind of rubs off on you. I remembered a little from when we were kids too."

"You always were better at it than me," I admitted and grimaced as I tried to get comfortable on the ground. Walter's magical goo was beginning to lose its potency, and the short walk had sapped my energy.

Santee asked me something with a concerned look on her face. She stood and left the tent suddenly. I turned to Dakota for an explanation. He just hiked his shoulders. Before I could wonder too long, Santee came back followed by several other women. They carried trays of what looked like the start of a meal. A kettle filled with something that smelled incredible was placed in the center of the floor, bowls and trays of bread sat next to it. Other bowls held fruit. A veritable feast. Our grandmother gestured to the food as the woman left us once more. My stomach growled, I didn't need to be told twice.

The kettle held a stew, I wasn't sure what the meat in it was, but I didn't really care. Scooping it up in a bowl, I grabbed a piece of bread and tried to remember my manners. Santee simply sat back and watched us eat, a satisfied smile on her face. I was shocked at how little my belly could hold. After half the bowl and a few bites of bread I was full.

"You haven't had anything solid in your stomach for a while, pal," Dakota told me. "Take it easy, okay?"

Dakota moved and knelt next to Santee and spoke softly to her, then bent down and kissed her lined face.

"I told her you had enough for your first day up, you needed to rest now."

"Yeah, a five-minute walk and a meal. My day is done," I said in disgust.

Dakota stood, and I took the hand he offered me. Santee got to her feet as well and moved next to me. Standing on her tiptoes, she pulled on my shirt, asking me to bend down. It hurt to do so, but I did it anyway. She placed a gentle kiss on my bruised face, paused for a moment and touched my cheek. Her hand moved to my chest, and she looked into my eyes.

"Montana Thomas," she said, in slow, halting English. "You are not ready for the spirits, not yet, not for a very long time. They have told me this. Go now." She gave me a small push with the hand on my chest. "Come back when you are rested."

When we were clear of the tent, I turned to Dakota. "She wasn't that scary," I told him.

"Oh yeah? Wait until she's pissed at something." He gave a little shudder. "She'll chill you to the bone, man, let me tell you."

Dakota took me by the arm and ushered me back to my tent. I was tired, but the last place I wanted to go was back to bed. I heard the sound of water off in the distance once again and remembered I had tried to get there once before.

"What is that, the water?" I asked my brother.

He stopped and listened, and then nodded in understanding. Growing up in a desert, waterfalls of any size or shape held a certain fascination for us. I convinced myself that was the source of the sound. Dakota confirmed it for me.

"Up the mountain a bit, one of the most beautiful falls I've ever seen. They get their water from a stream flowing down from it."

"I want to see it," I said and started off in the direction of the sound.

Dakota stood where he was and laughed at me. "No way, man. It's at least a mile hike, uphill. The going is steep and rocky. You wouldn't make it to the foothills in the condition you're in."

He was probably right, but I was so sick of everyone telling what I couldn't do, I kept walking, letting the sound guide me. I knew Dakota was following me, as long as he left me alone I didn't care. A minute into my walk, sweat covered me. My legs quivered as underused muscles objected to the sudden stress. I ignored what my body was trying to tell me and just kept moving.

There were no trails, no indication at all of which way to go. I turned around to find Dakota. "Which way?" I asked him, wiping sweat out of my eyes. I was breathing heavily, my ribs ached and my vision blurred, but I didn't care. Dakota seemed to understand.

"That way." He pointed to a small, almost invisible deer path heading directly up the steepest part of the mountain. I looked from Dakota to the path and back again. He just stayed where he was watching me.

I made it one, maybe two steps up the path before my foot slipped on a rock and I went down hard. Despite my best efforts to conceal it, I grunted with the pain and slid back down to the bottom. Determination won out over common sense, I ignored every warning signal my body was giving me and started again.

It was almost as if that hill and what waited for me on top symbolized everything I fought for, not just in the last month and not just for my life, but everything I had run from, or to. The lies I had thought my mother told me turned out to be nothing more than her way of doing what her husband, what my father, had asked of her. I realized that by ignoring her final plea, asking me to just let it go, I had accomplished exactly what she and my father had tried to prevent.

I had single-handedly brought my world crashing down around me, not only putting my life in jeopardy but an entire family I never knew I had. All because I could not just *let it go*!

My chest burned with every breath as mending bones were stressed to their limits. I pretended the pain wasn't there, and ignoring Dakota telling me to stop, I got to my feet again. My head started to spin and my vision blurred. I took one step and fell. Next time I tried, I only made it to my knees, but I didn't let that stop me. I crawled one step above where I had last fallen and collapsed, elated that I had at least beaten my personal best. In my mind the mountain had not beaten me yet.

I lay there gasping, trying to catch my breath, every bone and muscle in my body screaming, and a smile spread across my face despite it all.

"Are you done yet?" I looked up to find Dakota standing over me.

"For today, yeah, maybe. But I am going to get to the top of that mountain, Dakota, and when I do I am stripping naked and going for a swim in the pool at the bottom of those falls." I lay on my back with sweat rolling down my face, my head spinning, and I was happy. Dakota gave me a hand up.

"Your next challenge," he told me, "is making it back to camp, because I sure as hell am not carrying your sorry ass."

I stood, swayed, and Dakota's hand was immediately under my arm steadying me. "If I can't, you can leave me where I fall," I said.

"Deal." Dakota smiled.

I knew there was no way he would ever do that, but there was also no way I would let myself fall. I was on my way back, and I was fighting for every step.

CHAPTER 22

I became entirely single-minded in my obsession to get to that waterfall. Every day I would get up before the sun and start out. By the time I got to the foot of the mountain the morning sun would light my way. Clear, crisp air filled my lungs, and I found my muscles remembering their old strength with every step.

I knew someone was never far behind me. Dakota, my father or Tate followed me, staying just out of sight in the shadows. As long as they left me alone I ignored their presence. I couldn't blame them for their vigilance, and a part of me was grateful for it.

Every day it got easier, but like a carrot dangling from a stick, that damn waterfall eluded me and reminded me painfully of my fragile condition. I hated the weakness, I hated the body that no longer seemed like my own, but I was given no time for self-pity. When I wasn't trying to get to the top of that mountain to see my waterfall, Walter or my Santee put me to work. I wasn't stupid, *work* was therapy in disguise. Collecting firewood helped strengthen healing ribs and muscle as well as increase my endurance. Collecting water from the nearby stream, a few days ago an impossible task, was now difficult, but if I filled the kettle halfway, doable. The children outpaced me, laughing as they left me far behind. Some would shout at me as they ran past.

Wicaki! They called me—old man. I guess I was in their eyes, I know I felt like one. On the way back from the stream, one very hot day, I stopped to rest in the shade of a tree. I tried for a full bucket, and I attempted to carry it back to Santee's fire with my weak left arm. Before I made it a hundred feet, my muscles burned and when I ignored that warning they began to shake. The bucket spilled and all my hard work soaked into the ground at my feet.

"Son-of-a-bitch!" I kicked the empty bucket, and it tumbled back down toward the creek. I knew I would have to refill it, or Santee would just send me back anyway, turned out Dakota had been right about her being scary. But I didn't have it in me to do that just yet.

I leaned back against the tree and let the healing sun soothe me into a drowsy sleep. I woke with the strong sensation of someone watching me. At least my finely honed sixth sense hadn't completely abandoned me. When I was with the Rangers that little voice telling me something was out there kept me and my team alive.

There were no bad guys this time though, when I opened my eyes I found a boy sitting next to me. He couldn't have been more than ten. I looked around but he was alone, just sitting there shredding grass and leaning against the same tree as me. He was Native, his skin copper brown, his hair so black it almost looked blue in the sunlight.

I turned and gave him a quizzical look.

"Hi," he said and smiled.

"Who are you?" Most of the kids in camp were curious about me, but scattered when I got too close, too scared or too shy to talk to me, which was fine with me.

"I'm Noah. I filled your bucket for you."

I noticed the filled bucket sitting beside him. His arms looked like brittle toothpicks, I probably could have circled his bicep with my thumb and finger. I wondered how he managed to haul the heavy wooden bucket all the way back from the stream.

"So you did. Thanks."

"You need to give yourself a break you know."

I narrowed my eyes at him, confused by the comment. He didn't wait for me to say anything and explained himself. "I know you don't remember, but I helped take care of you a couple of times, sat with you when your brother needed to leave for a few moments every now and then." He turned and tilted his head to look up at me. "You talk in your sleep."

I raised my brows at that. "Did I say anything interesting?"

Noah considered the question. "No, you just mumbled."

"Sorry about that."

He shrugged. "It's okay. I'm glad you didn't die."

I grinned at that. "Me too, I think."

"See, that's what I mean—don't be so hard on yourself. I've watched you try to get to the top of the mountain. Every day at the same time you try. You look like it hurts so bad, but you never quit until you can't move anymore. I almost went to help you once, but thought you might be mad if I did."

"You followed me?" I knew someone always watched me, but thought it was my family.

"Sometimes, when someone else wasn't. I never saw anyone fight so hard for anything. I don't get it. What's at the top of that hill? Why's it so important that you nearly kill yourself all over again just to get there?"

I stared at the kid. "I don't know," I admitted. "Maybe I'm looking for who I used to be."

"And you think you'll find him at the top of a mountain?"

I hiked my shoulders. "It sounds stupid when you put it that way."

"Not stupid, but I can save you a lot of effort, you're not going to find who you were up there. That person doesn't exist anymore, the best you can do is try to figure out who you want to be, and then maybe be satisfied with who you are right now."

The lesson of a lifetime taught to me by a ten-year-old. I struggled to find something to say to that. "How'd you get so smart?"

"Grandpa Walt, well he's not my *real* grandpa, but he told me to call him that. He brought my mom and me here to live with him about a year ago. My dad was a drunk, he would hit me and my mom a lot. I tried to stop him, but I couldn't. I used to have a little brother, but one day he wouldn't stop crying, no matter what my mom did he just kept on crying—I think he was sick or something. Anyway, he woke my dad up and he was *pissed*. He took Nathan away from my mom and shook him so hard he died." Noah shrugged. "That's when Grandpa Walt took us here to live. It's better here. My mom smiles now."

I had no words for that. What could I possibly say to that?

Noah seemed to sense my uneasiness. "It's okay. I just wanted to let you know, I understand what it's like to lose yourself for a little while."

"Grandpa Walt?"

Noah grinned and stood. "I'd carry the water back for you, but Santee would not be happy."

I laughed softly at the honesty and the wisdom of one little boy. "No, she wouldn't."

Without another word, Noah turned and walked back toward camp, leaving me with a full bucket of water, a lighter heart, and words of wisdom to consider.

* * * *

The next morning, with a little boy's words fresh in my mind, I started up the mountain. I wondered if he watched and if he did, if he realized that today was the day. I knew my goal was within my grasp with the first step. I stood at the bottom of that deer path and looked up the steep incline. The sound of cascading water taunted me from the distance. Taking a deep breath, I pushed the hair from my eyes, vowing to get a haircut soon, even if I had to do it myself with a knife, then I started up that damn mountain.

By now I knew where all the loose rocks were and the ones I could use for leverage. My muscles moved smoothly beneath my flesh. I was still not on top of my game but so much better than I was. Not where I wanted to be, but it was a beginning for the search of who I had become, not for who I had been, maybe that made the difference.

I made it to the halfway point without stumbling once. I was sweating lightly, but it felt good. My breath came easily, there was no fatigue and no going back, not this time, not ever again. My ribs were still tender, but I smiled anyway as I pushed past the point where I had last been defeated. This mountain belonged to me now. The sound of water crashing down upon rocks grew louder as I breached the top of the hill. They were still out of sight, but I had made it. I had walked several steps before realizing I was no longer climbing, I was on level ground.

I turned and looked down where I had been. Nothing I had accomplished to that point in my life, not making the Rangers, not graduating law school, not even finding my father, felt as sweet as looking down that hill. It was a personal achievement I didn't think I would ever top.

Wiping a hand over my face, I silently saluted my worthy adversary, the mountain, then followed the sound of falling water to claim my reward. Tall pines, virgin stands of hemlock and pinions, marked the way. The trees gave way and showed me a sight that made the effort worthwhile.

Nestled among the craggy rocks and crevices of the mountain, the earth spewed forth her life's blood. Water collected from smaller tributaries far above me, joined into one larger stream, all constantly finding its path of least resistance and flowing downhill. With the ground suddenly removed, it fell over the side of the rocks to form a spectacular sight of cascading beauty that was beyond comparison. Mere words could not do it justice. The trees framed the gold and red of the rocks that served as a pathway for the water that held no color and every color at once.

Maybe twenty feet high, the pounding wall of water was deafening the closer I got to it. Making my way down to the pool at its bottom, I was careful on the wet, algae-slicked rocks at my feet. I might be feeling stronger than I was a week ago, but I was not stupid enough to believe myself immortal. One slip might put me right back in that hated tent, or worse, at Dakota's mercy once more. *That* was not happening.

Standing at the crystalline pool, I lifted my arms in gratitude for the simple gift of being alive to witness the sight before me. The spray from the falls settled lightly on my skin and clothes, and I remembered the promise I had made to Dakota that first day. Lifting my now less-than-clean shirt over my head and folding it carefully, I laid it on a boulder next to the water. Deciding the water would only help the wound on my arm, I took the dressing off and left the healing incision open to the air. Stepping out of my pants, I folded them and placed them next to the shirt. I just stood there naked, feeling the cool morning breeze as it caressed my body.

All the hurts I had suffered seemed far removed at that moment. Nothing could touch me here, no one could hurt me, I was invincible. I felt peace standing there on the edge of my world. I could feel my ancestors all around me, their presence a calming force. I was certain my mother was among them. It gave me an inner strength that I'd rarely experienced before. A strength I tried to remember so I could call on it in the future. For the first time in my life, I knew who I was—I was Lakota. I knew this was where I had come from; the strength of this place was infused into the very core of me. It was the calmness I had always craved from the desert, combined with a strength I never knew I possessed. This was a place where the demons could not find me, a place where I was safe. I was at peace.

Looking down into the crystalline depths, I judged the waters deep enough, climbed to the top of the boulder hanging over the edge of the pool, and dove in.

The chill of the mountain streams shocked my system and took my breath. I surfaced in a noisy spray and then as the water numbed my body, I found I could breathe again. I skirted to the edge of the whirlpool near the base of the falls and discovered I could actually sneak behind the pounding wall of water. It was hypnotic, I stayed there sitting in the shallow rock-strewn basin, watching and thinking. I felt like the only person alive on the face of the earth. I liked the feeling.

I realized I was shivering and decided the illusion needed to end. With regret, I left the security of the falls and swam in slow, lazy strokes to the edge of the pool and pulled myself out. Naked, dripping, cold and a little blue, I must have been quite the sight. I forgot about my invisible bodyguard, until I heard the voice behind me. I tried not to jump at the unexpected sound.

"You look like you're freezing."

I turned to find my father standing just behind me, holding my clothes out to me. I breathed a sigh of relief that it hadn't been Tate's turn to follow me today. I took my pants and pulled them up over my hips, the soft leather warm from the early morning sun.

"A little," I told him. "I don't mind, it reminds me that I'm still alive."

"You look good, Montana."

I shook my head. "I have a long way to go to get to where I was."

"But you've come a long way from where you were," he reminded me, then took a seat on the boulder looking out over the falls. "I used to come here all the time as a kid," he said. "Made me feel like the only person alive in the world."

I smiled as he mirrored my own thoughts, but said nothing.

"I'm sorry," he said after a long silence.

The apology took me off guard. "For what?" I asked, coming to stand next to him.

He shrugged, looking out at the water forever falling. "For not being there for you when you were growing up, for not being a father to you, or a husband to Lilly. Sorry for the decisions that made that necessary. Sorry my past nearly got you killed." He almost seemed as if he were talking to himself. He never looked at me, just at the water, as if by wishing it hard enough he could rewind time and change his past.

I pulled the shirt over my head, pleased when the movement didn't cause too much pain in my arm. I shook the water from my hair and worked up the courage to ask him the one question I'd asked myself since I discovered who he was.

"Was it worth it, Dad?" I didn't mean to be accusing or condemning, I honestly wanted to know if he thought what he had done was justified. I still wasn't convinced it had been.

The question got his attention and he turned to face me. "I swore I would never do this," he said.

"Do what? Explain yourself?"

"No, justify myself to you."

"It's just a question, Dad. No justification needed. I mean, I get it, you took money, a lot of money. Enough to be killed for, so you ran and made yourself and your family disappear. I only wanted to know if the money was worth it, worth not getting to know your sons, worth your wife's sanity, worth our lives." *Now* I was accusing and condemning. Now I wanted him to answer me.

"Worth all of that?" He sighed and shook his head slowly. "What do you want me to say, Montana? You've already condemned me, made yourself judge and jury, does it matter what the reasons were? Would it change how you feel about me?"

"I won't know that until I hear the reasons."

David looked back out at the falls. He looked tired, as if life had caught up with him all at once. "I grew up with a kid on one of the reservations, before my father started all of this. His name was William One Horse. We were best friends from the time we could both walk. He had big dreams, wanted to be a doctor, come back here and treat the people for free."

He had a faraway look as he spoke. I couldn't figure out how it related to the question, but I let him get to it in his own way.

"That was before he discovered alcohol," David continued. "I knew he had a problem by the time we were twelve or thirteen. He would steal money from his old man just to score a fifth and hide somewhere to down it. At first he asked me to join him, but after helping him polish off a bottle of cheap whiskey and spending the next day puking my guts out, I'd had enough—never touched another drop. The same could not be said of William."

"What happened to him?" I asked.

"He drank himself to death by the time he was twenty." David turned to me. "Do you know what it is like to see someone you love slowly kill themself and feel helpless to do anything about it? He had so much potential, and he drowned it in a bottle before it ever had a chance to grow. I stole that money to give kids like him a choice, to give them a chance at a decent education. William knew he was never going to go to college, his folks couldn't afford it. He found his way out of the res all right." David took a slow, deep breath and put the memory away. "Was it worth it?" He shrugged. "I really don't know. At the time I thought it was. I didn't realize what I did would cost me a future with my family. Can you understand that even a little?"

"Yeah, I guess I can. But you can't tell me you didn't keep some of it for yourself."

"Some of it, sure, I kept some. Set up secured accounts for you and Dakota, so you could both go to school and do whatever you wanted. I made sure Lilly would never want for a thing as long as she lived. The rest went to the college funds, an anonymous donation. Some I gave to my father so he could do this, and later I gave him more so he could keep it going." He gestured to the encampment down the mountain. "I funded his clinic, paid for food and clothing for some of the ones who were barely making it." He shrugged and turned away again.

Adding it all up in my head, I took a step toward my father. "Dad, exactly how much money are we talking about here? Everything you've funded for almost thirty years now, not counting the money Mom gave for the library in Ekalaka, that's a hell of a lot of money."

He turned to me and locked his eyes on mine. "Yeah, it is. So you tell me, Montana, was it worth it? I've been trying to figure that out most of my life. Sometimes I convince myself it was. Watching what it has done to you, all my rationale disappears. I knew I couldn't hide forever, but the more time that went by, the more I thought I just might have done it, I might have eluded my past and the bastards looking for my blood. Never once did I consider it would be you who found me." He almost smiled at that. "Never once did I consider the danger I put you in by having Lilly keep the truth from you."

I looked out at the water with him, the sound soothing and demanding at once. A realization came to me. "This isn't over, is it?" I asked, even though I already knew the answer.

"No, not by a long shot. We can't stay here. It's not safe for the people in the camp. I wasn't thinking when I made the decision to contact my father. He took great pains to keep this place hidden from the rest of the world. He owns the land and the mountain we're standing on, I made sure of that as well. But all I could think about that night was 'my son is dying.'"

Cocking my head toward him, I tried to figure out what he wasn't telling me. "Exactly what are you saying, Dad?"

"I called my father. He has a cellphone, never uses it, but he has patients who call him from time to time, so he keeps it on."

"The call was traceable," I concluded.

My father nodded and sighed. Scrubbing a hand over his face, he told me the rest. "Yeah, that and I left a trail a blind man could follow. I drove my Range Rover, Tate followed in your Jeep. We left them just down the hill from the encampment. I did what I could to cover our trail, bought us some time, but we need to leave. Whoever is calling the shots at the casino these days is going to find us if we stay." My father looked at me and made sure I was listening to what he was saying. "They are coming for us, Montana."

"You should have left me," I said, never realizing the danger he had put these people in by bringing me here to save my life.

"I left you once, never again. Besides, even after telling my father everything, he would never let me move you."

I just stared at him, uncomprehending. "We have to leave here, now!" I said. It felt as if every moment counted.

"I know, that's what I wanted to talk to you about today. I was waiting for you to get stronger. I would like to wait a little longer, but we don't have the time."

"God, Dad, my life isn't worth putting this entire camp at risk. I can't be responsible for that." All I could think about was my grandparents, the children, Noah, all the people who put their trust in my grandfather. It was all at risk because they opened their home up to me.

"You aren't responsible for that, I am."

"I'm not worth all of that." I couldn't believe what my father and my grandfather had done for me.

My father jumped down off the boulder and reached out to touch me. For some reason he pulled his hand back at the last moment, as if he thought I wouldn't welcome the contact.

"Yes, you are, Montana. Yes, you are."

The simple statement was about as selfish as anything I had ever heard and more touching than I could have possibly imagined. It was a father declaring he would do anything to keep his son safe. I had no words to give him in return. I only hoped he understood my silence for what it was. Gratitude, respect and hell, yes, love.

As much as I wanted to keep the anger I had harbored all my life alive and kicking, the reality of the situation was I loved my father, I always had. I loved him when my mother told me stories about him. I loved him even when I tried to hate him. I loved him when I sat in the cool of the desert night listening for him in the songs of the coyotes.

CHAPTER 23

The walk back down the mountain was infinitely easier than climbing up. I should have been exhausted, and I suppose on some level I was, but despite the urgency I felt a sense of peace. I had reached a truce with myself and my feelings for my father. I realized that I had forgiven him. With that knowledge in hand, anything was possible. I only wished my mother could have witnessed this moment. She deserved the peace I had found here. I spent a lifetime searching for happiness, looking for peace. I chased stories, dreams, addictions and even other people hoping to fill the emptiness that plagued me. The irony is the only place I ever needed to look was inside me. I stood in the center of my circle and I was home.

Too bad the revelation came too late to do me much good.

My father and I kept up quiet conversation on the way back to the camp. When we were about a hundred yards away from the clearing opening up to the camp, he put an arm out stopping me.

"What?" I asked.

He put a finger to his lips, asking for silence, and then canted his head as he listened. Confusion and concern painted his features. I felt it too, something was wrong, but I wasn't as tuned in to it as my father.

"What is it?" I whispered.

"What do you hear?"

Pausing for a moment, I realized the mountain was quiet. There was no sounds of children playing, woman working, people going about the ordinary everyday routine of life, even the birds were silent. It was if the entire mountain held its breath and waited for release.

"Nothing," I told my father. "I hear nothing." My expression must have mirrored his own.

"We stayed too long," David said. "They found us."

Creeping up to the tree line so the camp was in view, we both surveyed the clearing.

"Where is everyone?" I whispered.

"I don't know, it looks deserted."

Sudden movement from the center of camp caused both of us to look in that direction. A tall man with short blond hair left one of the tents. As he ducked to fit through the low doorway, I got a good look at his face. I'd never seen him before. Judging by the look on my father's face, the same could not be said of him.

"Who is that?" I asked, but before he could answer, the tent flap opened once more. This time I did recognize one of the faces. Two men dragged a third between them. The man in the middle could barely walk, his head hung on his chest, blood flowed from his nose and mouth. I recognized Dakota beaten and barely conscious as the men on either side of him threw him to the ground. He rolled in the dirt, and then lay still where he landed.

Without thinking, I got to my feet. David pulled me down hard.

"They have my brother!" I turned on him. My gut reaction was to protect Dakota.

"And they have my son," David countered. "Think a minute, Montana. We're unarmed." He motioned to the men in the clearing, they now numbered six. "They aren't. You're not going to help Dakota rushing in there and being stupid. We need a plan."

I watched as the men who had thrown Dakota on the ground bent to retrieve him once more. They held ropes in their hands now. One of them squatted down next to him and lifted his head up by his hair.

"Wakey, wakey, Chief." He laughed. Together with his helper they got Dakota to his feet and dragged him over to a deer tree. Two poles with a cross bar between them. In the center was a winch used to haul deer up for butchering. No deer today, just Dakota.

They tied his wrists together and looped them over the hook at the bottom of a rope, then slowly winched him up until he hung just inches off the ground. Dakota stirred as his weight settled on his wrists. His eyes opened, but they were unfocused and glazed with pain.

The blond man stood in front of Dakota and held his arms out. "Ollie Ollie oxen free, Jake! Come out, come out, wherever you are!"

"You know him?" I couldn't take my eyes from Dakota.

"Yeah," my father answered in a low voice. "I know him."

In the clearing, the blond man spoke over his shoulder to one of his men near Dakota. His voice carried to where we watched.

"Cut him," he said.

One of the men, a big guy with a buzzcut, walked next to Dakota and withdrew a knife from a sheath at his hip.

"Jake, I know you're out there, and I know you're listening to me. I found the vehicles, Jake. Damn, that was a lot of blood. I'm thinking son number one didn't fair too well. Want to go two for two?" Blond man laughed and gave the go ahead to Buzzcut.

"No way," I said, realizing what they planned on doing. I tried to get to my feet again, and my father pulled me down once more. "They're going to kill him!"

"And they already think you're dead!" he reminded me. "What do you think you're going to do, Montana? Give them another chance at you? You can't help Dakota, but I might be able to."

In the clearing Buzzcut took the knife and slit the material of Dakota's shirt, baring his chest.

"Listen to me," David said urgently. "My father and the camp are out there, count on that. Wait for them. If you follow me, you'll only get Dakota killed."

Buzzcut took the knife and slowly drew it across the flesh of Dakota's chest. The cut was shallow, a thin stream of blood flowed from the wound. Dakota's face pinched up in pain. He let out a low cry, and his hands bunched around the ropes that held him. I couldn't take my eyes from the sight.

"Montana!" My father turned me toward him, demanding my attention. "Do you understand me?"

"You're going to them?" I asked. I couldn't believe he would do that. After all the years of hiding he would so easily give himself up to these men.

"It will buy Dakota time. Wait for my father." Without another word, he left my side and walked out of the trees toward the clearing.

I couldn't believe what was happening. My brother was hung up like fresh meat, my father was walking to the proverbial lion's den, and there I sat doing nothing. As the shock finally wore off, I shook my head at my own ineptness.

"No way," I said to no one and found my feet. I was not abandoning Dakota and letting my father walk in there unarmed. I knew firsthand what these men were capable of. I'd had enough of being their victim.

A hand on my shoulder pushed me back down to my knees. Without thinking, I turned on the intruder and threw a punch in what I hoped was the direction of his face.

My grandfather deflected the intended punch easily and in one smooth move, pushed me to my back with a foot.

"Save it," he whispered to me. "You'll need that anger later."

I wanted to ask him what had happened, what about my father, what about Dakota, what was he planning to do, but I couldn't get the words out. Instead, I gave one last look at Dakota, then took my grandfather's offered hand and followed him deep into the trees surrounding us.

CHAPTER 24

"How many are there?" I asked, ducking under branches and following my surprisingly spry grandfather through the trees.

"Just the six. One shotgun, the rest have handguns. It's not a problem."

"It's not a problem? How can you say it's not a problem? They have Dakota. How the hell did they get Dakota?" I yelled to my grandfather's back. I was having a little difficulty keeping up with him and despite the adrenaline zinging through my system, I was feeling lightheaded.

"Your brother was worried about you. My scouts radioed up to alert us that we were about to have unwelcome guests. We left to get the women and children to safety. Dakota insisted on going back to warn you." My grandfather stopped and turned around to look at me. "I tried to stop him."

"So you just let them take him?" I couldn't believe he would do that. That he would watch his own flesh and blood beaten in front of him.

My grandfather shook his head. "I haven't lived this long by being stupid, Montana. I am not about to let that vermin infest my home. Look around you, what do you see?"

I couldn't get the picture of Dakota hanging beaten and bloodied in that clearing out of my head, so when I looked the first time, all I saw were the trees surrounding us, then suddenly something made me take a closer look.

My eyes adjusted to the dim light and picked out shadows within the shadows. Lining the perimeter of the tree line were the men from my grandfather's camp, looking like a flashback from a century or more past. Bare chests and faces painted with the colors of the forest, they were camouflage perfected. Armed with dangerous longbows and quivers filled with hand fletched arrows, they looked like their ancestors. Like *my* ancestors.

Fifty or more strong, able-bodied men surrounded the clearing where my father and Dakota were now being held. My grandfather was right, it didn't matter how well the intruders were armed, the odds had just shifted considerably in our favor.

"What are you waiting for?" I asked, looking back through the trees at the camp as the man drew the blade across Dakota's chest once more. "Stop him!"

"I'm waiting to hear from my scouts," my grandfather told me. "If more are coming, or we missed some, these people could be killed. These men have families. I will not risk their lives needlessly."

"But you would risk Dakota's," I said. I could hear Dakota's screams echo through the hills. It took everything I had to just sit there and have a conversation with my grandfather as my brother was being tortured.

"Have patience, my son knows what to do."

"Not real big on patience here, Walt."

"I noticed that about you." My grandfather's hand went to an earpiece he wore. I hadn't noticed that before. I recognized it as a communication device not very different from the ones I had used in the Rangers. The clash of technology and Native culture was once again a little unsettling.

The message apparently received, my grandfather said nothing but swung the impossibly long bow from where it had rested on his back and drew out an arrow from the fully loaded quiver there. He smoothed the feathers along the shaft with two fingers and gave me a sideways glance.

"We wait," he said.

Together we waited and watched as my father gave himself over to his own demons.

* * * *

My father entered the clearing where Dakota hung like a deer ready for butchering. And I watched as he became someone he used to be. He ceased being David Willows and became Jacob Willowcreek before my eyes.

Before he got ten feet into the clearing he was tackled hard from behind, a knee shoved in the center of his back, his arms wrenched behind him. He was pulled to his feet and dragged to where the blond man stood waiting for him with a satisfied smile on his face. Their voices carried to me through the trees by the wind.

"Let him go," Blond Man told his men. "Been a long time, Jake."

"Not long enough, Mike," my father said, as the men holding him released him with a shove.

Blond Man, newly christened Mike, spread his arms and looked hurt at the comment. "Ah, Jake, what, you didn't miss me? That hurts, truly cuts me to the bone. I missed you, Jake. Been looking for you. Got to give you credit though, man, you played one hell of a game of hide-and-seek." Mike put a friendly arm around my father's shoulders and walked with him to where Dakota hung.

I could just make out the look on David's face as he looked up at Dakota. He had regained consciousness, but still looked a little dazed.

He pulled and tugged against the ropes that held him.

"David?" He sounded as if he wasn't sure who he saw.

"Nice looking boy you have there, Jake. I can see that pretty wife of yours in him. Oh, my condolences, by the way." A look of mock sympathy played across Mike's face and then was gone in an instant, replaced by impatience and outrage.

"Guess what, Jakey? Game's over." Mike motioned to the man with the knife. With one quick flick of the blade, he cut Dakota along his jaw and as my brother moved and yelled with the pain, the blade slipped and moved to his throat. Blood spilled down his neck and chest.

"I killed one son, I can take this one piece by piece if I have to."

Another crimson streak appeared on the other side of Dakota's jaw. Dakota twisted and cried out in pain. He kicked weakly at his tormentor, but never got close to the man with the knife.

David took a step forward and was held back by Mike's hand on his chest and the threat of the knife at Dakota's throat. It took everything I had to stay where I was and watch what they did to my family.

"You shut me down for ten years, Jake. Your little anonymous tip to the authorities brought the FBI to my doorstep. I had to play by the rules. You shut me down you son-of-a-bitch!" Mike pushed David hard. He stumbled back a step or two but stayed on his feet. "I want my money, Jake. I want my God damn, fucking money!" Mike shoved again, harder, and I could see him struggle to control his temper. I knew then the man would kill my father and my brother if nothing, no one, stopped him.

I watched as the man my father called Mike smoothed down the leather vest and adjusted the collar of his denim shirt. He looked a little out of his element, like a misplaced city boy transplanted to the country.

"You look like you just stepped out of an L.L. Bean catalog," David said as if reading my thoughts. I thought he might be trying to buy Dakota some time, and I looked to my grandfather for permission to enter the clearing.

Walter shook his head once. "Not yet."

I looked at him with frustration. I knew the knife strikes to Dakota were going to start getting more deadly. I had no delusions that Mike intended to let Dakota leave the clearing alive. I had to trust that Walter would never let it get that far.

"Hey, I can be flexible, but man, why the hell would you want to live all the way out here?" Mike asked my father. "I don't get the allure, Jake, I really don't. And nice family you have, by the way. They took off running the moment they heard us coming. Yeah, big, fucking brave Indians." Mike laughed and his henchman laughed with him. Mike pulled a gun from the waistband of his pants and patted the barrel lovingly. "Right here is the reason we beat their asses. Superior fire power, my man. You cannot argue with superior fire power."

"Custer was defeated at Little Bighorn by five hundred Indians with bows and arrows," David reminded him.

All the humor drained from Mike's face. "Well, this ain't fucking Little Bighorn and I ain't fucking Custer." Mike took the knife from the man at Dakota's side and settled it under his chin.

I tried to jump to my feet, but Walter's hand on my shoulder kept me still.

"You've had almost thirty years to invest *my* money, Jake. I figure that's almost a hundred percent growth on my investment. I want the whole hundred mil plus thirty years' worth of interest wired to a secured account, or I bleed your boy dry and you get to watch. It's going to get messy, pal." Mike moved the point of the blade from Dakota's chin to his chest and pushed the blade home, no shallow cut this time.

Dakota screamed and writhed as metal met bone, the shaft of the knife hitting his sternum. Mike withdrew the bloodied blade and turned to Jake.

"I want your numbered accounts and the passwords to gain access." Mike gave a nod to one of his men who withdrew a laptop from a bag over his shoulder. "Now," Mike told my father. "Or the next time, I hit something he might need."

"You'll never get reception out here," David said. I could see the effort it took for him to tear his eyes from Dakota and force himself to deal with Mike.

Mike only grinned as his man fired up the computer. "Satellite signal," he explained. "I have connections. Give him the numbers, Jake, and don't give me any bullshit about not knowing them. I figure a man in your position would not leave a paper trail. You have the numbers right here." Mike tapped the side of his head.

David shook his head. "Give me a minute, I can't remember them."

"Think fast." Mike put the knife against the crook of Dakota's arm tied above his head. "Brachial artery lies right about there. I nick that, I figure he's got ten, maybe fifteen minutes until he bleeds out." He pressed the knife against Dakota's skin just hard enough to draw blood.

Dakota's eyes were wide with the beginnings of shock, but he was still with it. He met our father's eyes and shook his head. "He'll kill me anyway," he said. "Don't give him anything."

"Oh, God, now, see that's freaking touching. Almost brought a tear to my eye." In one quick movement, Mike brought the knife down along the inside of Dakota's left arm. He stepped back quickly, but failed to avoid the arterial spray as the blade hit home. "No more games, Jake. You've got ten minutes before your son bleeds to death."

My grandfather touched my arm and I forced myself to look away from Dakota and meet his eyes.

"Now," he said.

Before David could move, before Dakota's scream of pain stopped echoing through the trees, the man at the computer slumped to the ground, dead, an arrow shaft buried deep in his back. Walter's people had obviously received the same message.

David took a step toward Dakota as Mike's men went on alert, firing their guns blindly at unseen adversaries.

"What the fuck?" Mike looked at his man lying dead on the ground. "What the fuck!"

A moment later he dropped the knife as the hand that held it became impaled with an arrow through the palm. My attention went from the scene in the clearing to the woods surrounding me as war cries that had not been heard for over a century echoed through the air and a hail of deadly fire volleyed through the clearing.

Confused and disoriented by the sudden unexpected attack, Mike's men fired randomly into the trees. Their shots were wild and panicked. It was clear they were used to one-sided battles against unarmed opponents.

David claimed the dropped knife and cut the rope holding Dakota up. He fell to the ground with a thud, as David rushed forward. Arrows and bullets cut the air around him.

Frozen and unarmed, I watched Mike hold his hand by the wrist, writhing in agony. Blood, both his and Dakota's, splattered his new clothes. Somehow I didn't think this was what L.L. Bean intended when he suggested his clothes were made for rugged wear.

Rolling Dakota over onto his back, David cut the ropes binding his wrists and leaned all his weight over the severed artery spewing precious blood onto the ground. Dakota was conscious, but his face was pale and his eyes glazed.

"Hang on, pal," I heard my father tell Dakota as I finally came out of my stupor. "I think the Indians are going to win this one for a change."

"Now," my grandfather repeated. "Now is the time to release that anger you try so hard to control." Holding the bow and arrow in one hand, he withdrew a six-inch-long Bowie knife from a leather sheath at his boot and handed it to me. "I don't think your arm is strong enough for a bow yet, but I believe you might make some use of this."

I took the knife and gave him a nod.

"Montana?"

I looked up at him.

"There can be no survivors. Do you understand?"

"Wasn't planning on any," I told him and clenched my hand around the hilt of the weapon as Dakota's screams cut through the air once more.

Racing into the clearing, I was well behind the initial surge. I caught a brief glimpse of my father kneeling over Dakota, all I could register was blood, I couldn't tell who it belonged to. My guess, judging from the screams I had heard, would be Dakota.

Instinct made me want to go to my father's side, to see how badly Dakota was hurt, meticulous training had me searching for the bad guys and neutralizing all existing threats. Mike was on the ground clutching his hand with the arrow through his palm. All I could think was *good, he's not dead yet.* Someone had seen fit to grace me with the gift of taking the bastard down.

Everything slowed as I ran the few feet across that clearing. This was the man who had taken my father away from me, the man who had taken my mother's husband, the love of her life away. The man who had ordered Lilly Thomas beaten in front of her husband and witnessed by a two-year-old boy, who told no one he remembered. He remembered everything. *I* remembered everything.

Somewhere in the back of my mind, I heard war cries echo across a land that was no stranger to blood being split upon it. Finding strength in the pain of my healing body, I charged the man responsible for my demons, determined to kill him over and over again.

Running full tilt, I dove, leading with my feet. My heels found their mark on his chin and sent him sprawling onto his back. He landed dazed and vulnerable. I didn't care. It didn't matter he was unarmed, it didn't matter he was injured and unable to defend himself. I let the darkness I never allowed come to the surface completely consume me.

I heard a cry of rage come from inside me as I stood over the man and lifted his head by the hair. I didn't hesitate, I took the knife and slit the side of his throat. Sweet, warm blood gushed from the wound and covered me. I welcomed it.

I was someone I wouldn't have recognized. Covered in my enemy's blood and screaming war cries I'd never heard before, I wasn't satisfied with simply killing the man. I plunged the knife again and again into his now lifeless body until there was nothing recognizably human left. Then in a completely savage act, I stood over the body and took my trophy. The impeccably sharp edge of the Bowie knife had no difficulties separating the man from his scalp. Blond hair, now glistening red and dripping blood, was held aloft for all to see.

I had no idea how long the demons had control over me. I cannot deny the fact that I killed an unarmed man, I simply had no clear memory of consciously doing it. Yes, I remember the knife plunging into his body, but it was almost as if I was watching someone else do it and I was on the side lines urging him on. *Again! Again! Again!*

I came back to myself and collapsed to my knees, still holding the bloody piece of hair I had cut from the man's head. I lowered my arm, and the rest of the clearing came into focus for me.

They were all dead, all six of them. Not one of my grandfather's people had been touched. They stood much like I did, covered in blood, elated and exhausted at the victory. This was not like the battles I had been in before. I had killed men before, on orders, for my country, for a political agenda. This was different and far more personal. I killed now to protect my family only a few feet away, to survive, to avenge a lost childhood, to make peace with the beast they had created inside of me.

My grandfather came beside me and took the knife from my hand. He looked at the bloody thing that had once been a person lying at my feet and simply nodded.

"It is good they are dead," he said. 'They had no honor."

I dropped the scalp and remembered Dakota for the first time. I ran over to where my father still knelt over him. My brother was covered in almost as much blood as I was, the difference being, most of it was his own.

My father leaned with all his weight on Dakota's arm. Dakota's face was pale beneath the blood and pinched with pain.

"How is he?" I asked, coming to kneel next to my father.

My father turned his head in my direction and I watched him take in everything, then keeping his eyes on mine, he adjusted the grip he had on Dakota's arm. Dakota let out a small cry of pain.

"Bastard cut his artery, he's bleeding out. I have pressure on it, but I think the son-of-a-bitch severed it."

"Can he be moved?" I asked.

My grandfather knelt on the other side of my father and shook his head. "He's lost too much blood, if Jacob lets go, it could kill him." Sliding a leather cord beneath Dakota's arm and above the injury, my grandfather prepared to tie a tourniquet.

Dakota shook his head in objection. I was amazed he was still conscious.

"No," he reached over and put his right hand on my grandfather's.

"Dak, what, why?" I asked.

My grandfather answered for him. "The tourniquet will most likely save his life—"

"Then do it!" I interrupted. I didn't get why he was hesitating or why Dakota was objecting.

"But then the blood supply to his arm will be cut off. Unless circulation can be restored within twenty minutes—give or take—he will lose the arm."

"Dak, it's your life we're talking about. Come on," I said.

The sound of helicopter blades cutting through the pristine air almost didn't register with me.

"He doesn't need to make that decision," Grandfather said.

He tied a knot around a stick and twisted it tightly over Dakota's bicep. Dakota let out a scream that sent the birds from their perches in the trees above us, then mercifully he went slack under my father's hands, the shock and pain finally taking over.

"I used their own satellite signal," Grandfather explained. "That is a medi-vac helicopter, they'll get Dakota to Billings in time. Tell them when I put the tourniquet on. Get him to your vehicle and meet them at the bottom of the mountain."

"What about all of this?" my father asked, indicating the carnage all around him.

"It will be taken care of," came the answer. "There is no one left to hurt you now. Take care of your son, Jacob."

I bent down to help lift Dakota when my grandfather stopped me. "You can't go with them," he told me. "There would be too many questions and not enough answers. Do you understand?"

I did, but I didn't like it. I wanted to be with Dakota. I *needed* to be with him, but I was covered in another man's blood and surrounded by bodies that could not be explained.

"What will you tell them?" I asked my father, meaning Dakota's injuries.

Lifting my unconscious brother in his arms, my father spared me a glance before starting the hike down the mountain toward the medi-vac and civilization.

"I'll come up with something," he said over his shoulder, then he glanced at Grandfather, a look passing between them. "I'll call you when we get there."

"Wait." I ran over to Dakota, lying in my father's arms. Placing a hand on his face, I told myself this would not be the last time I saw him. "Come back, man," I said. "I still have payback to exert."

I thought I saw the hint of a smile on his face, but then it could have been wishful thinking on my part. I took my hand back and left a bloody smear where I had touched him. I watched my father disappear with him as the helicopter swooped in low to land at the bottom of the trail.

Looking at my hands for the first time, I let my eyes follow a trail down the rest of me. I saw a nightmare washed in red. I understood what my grandfather meant when he said I would only generate more questions than answers.

I was suddenly exhausted and went down on my knees, my body having the final say. I sat surrounded by the dead. The battle over, the enemy defeated.

Why then was I having trouble figuring out exactly what it was I'd won?

CHAPTER 25

Blood is an amazing thing. It is life. The human body contains roughly six quarts of the precious stuff, looks like a hell of a lot more when it is spilt. Warm, it has the consistency of milk, cold it is very much like syrup, sticky and congealing. It smells a lot like burned honey, kind of sweet. Funny, I never considered blood having an aroma before.

We piled the bodies in the center of the clearing. My grandfather poured animal fat used for cooking over the mound and set fire to them. In silence the whole of the camp, bloodied warriors, women and children alike, watched them burn. It was a gruesome, almost hypnotic sight. The wind carried the smell away from us for now, but it would linger for days.

I had no desire to listen to the hissing and crackling of human flesh as the fires consumed its feast. I stumbled down to the creek and waded in the cold waters, trying to remove the blood from my body. The beautiful clothes Santee had made for me were beyond any hope of repair. I peeled the once pristine white shirt over my head and threw it to the ground. It was nearly black with the gore that covered it.

Suddenly desperate to remove the blood from my skin, I splashed water over me and scrubbed and tried to wash myself clean, but it wouldn't come off. I knew my movements had become frantic, almost manic in nature. I didn't care, I scrubbed until it hurt, but the blood still wouldn't come off. I concentrated on my hands and tried to work the blood out of the crevices around my fingernails and knuckles.

All I could see was Dakota lying on the ground covered in his own blood.

"My fault, my fault." The thoughts became words I wasn't aware of verbalizing. Standing half naked in the ice of the mountain stream, trying to wash a dead man's blood off my hands while wondering if my brother was even still alive, I didn't hear Tate come up behind me.

"Montana?"

I whirled at the sound of her voice and laughed when I saw her standing calf deep in the water behind me. She must have been freezing, but her face showed only concern.

"I shouldn't have let him come," I said. The smile on my face was wholly inappropriate, but I couldn't seem to help it. "He should be in school, he should be staying up all night worrying over finals and what hospitals he's going to do his residencies at." I showed my hands to Tate. "I can't get it off," I told her and shook my head. "I tried, but I can still see it. Can't you see it, Tate?" She looked at me in confusion, and I wondered how she couldn't see the blood, I was covered in it. I *needed* to get it *off!* I had to get it *off!*

Falling to my knees in the stream, I splashed the water over me until I was saturated and shivering and started the frantic scrubbing again. When that didn't work, I used my nails to try and scrape it off.

"Montana, stop!" Tate ran over and grabbed my hands in hers. "Stop," she begged, and I noticed for the first time she was crying. I didn't understand why and I didn't want her to touch me, I didn't want the blood to get on her. I tried to take my hands from hers, but she held on tightly.

"No, it will get on you," I told her.

"I'll help you," Tate said, pulling on my hands. "Let me help you.

God, you're freezing."

I let her lead me from the stream and wondered if I was. I couldn't feel anything.

"Can you get it off?" I asked her.

"Yeah, hun, come back with me. Warm water and soap will help. Come on back with me."

I followed her out of the stream and let her lead me back to the camp. The women and older children were already setting things right. Noah was there, I met his eyes, his looked wounded and I wanted to know what he had seen. I saw water boiling in kettles on several fires. Tate led me to a tent on the far side of the camp, as far away from the sight of the carnage as possible. Inside Santee and a few other women were waiting.

Without a word they motioned me to sit. It didn't occur to me to object when Tate and my grandmother began washing me. The water was hot and when it touched my skin, only then did I realize how cold I was.

They worked in silence and I closed my eyes and let them. Gentle, diligent hands washed the blood from my hair, my body, but they could not begin to touch the stains on my soul. I felt hands tug on the drawstring to my pants and stopped them. Opening my eyes, I shook my head at Santee and tried to smile.

"I can take it from here," I said, hoping for a little privacy. She nodded and motioned for the rest of the women to leave.

Tate stayed behind for a moment. She pointed to a pile of clothes in the corner. "I wasn't sure of the size, so there are a couple of different ones. Just see which fits best."

"Where did you get them?"

"Cousins, uncles." She shrugged. "You needed something to wear."

I picked up a flannel shirt and rubbed the material between my fingers. The water might have warmed my body, but I still felt as if I were shivering on the inside.

"You always seem to be there to save me," I said quietly. "Tate, what the hell did I do?"

"What you had to. You did exactly what you had to do, we all did." She turned to leave me alone and called back over her shoulder. "Finish dressing, we have a long drive ahead of us."

I snapped my head up at that. "David called?"

She nodded. "Dakota's in surgery. I figured you would want to be there when he wakes up." She ducked under the tent flap and left me alone.

You did what you had to do.

Did I? I didn't have to find my father, I didn't have to follow the lead that Sam Blackcrow gave me, and I sure as hell didn't have to involve Dakota.

I looked down at my hands, I knew they were clean, they had done good work, even my nails were clean. Not one drop of blood to be seen. Why then, could I only see the red?

* * * *

I found a t-shirt and jeans that fit reasonably well, and my sneakers at the bottom of the pile. Tate had even thought of socks. I passed on the underwear though. Seemed a little too much like using someone else's toothbrush. I slipped on the denim jacket I had been wearing at Medicine Rocks, to ward against the chill that still seeped through me, and met Tate in the clearing. I tried to avoid looking at the fire still crackling and popping in the center and walked to where she spoke with my grandfather.

"You spoke to David?" I asked, when I got his attention.

"Yes, I gave Tate directions. I spoke with the surgeons. They are confident Dakota will have full use of his arm. He got to surgery with time to spare."

"You're not coming with us?" I asked.

My grandfather took a step toward me and shook his head. "I'm needed here. We will be moving the camp."

"I'm sorry," I said. It took everything I had to look him in the eye. "I brought this here." I couldn't take his scrutiny any longer and finally looked away to the fire burning brightly. "I'm sorry," I said again. It seemed like such a useless thing to say. I hoped he knew I meant the words. I would have done anything to take it all back, to have the chance to start over.

"You are sorry for what? For finding a family you never knew you had? Or are you sorry for surviving, or perhaps you are sorry for killing the man who wanted to kill you and your brother?" My grandfather turned my face to meet his. "These are not things to be sorry over. This is just the way of life."

"It isn't quite what I expected," I said.

"Life seldom is. Let me share something that has taken me a long time to figure out," my grandfather said. "For a long time, it seemed to me that life was about to begin, my real life, but there was always something in the way. Some obstacle to overcome, something that needed to be completed first. It seemed I must get these things done first and then my life could begin. At last it dawned on me, that these obstacles were my life. In the book of life, every page has two sides. We human beings fill one side with our hopes and dreams, our plans and wishes, but providence writes on the other side of the page, and what it ordains is seldom what we wish for."

"I didn't think of the consequences, Grandfather. I didn't think about anything except what I wanted. I dragged Dakota into this, my father, Tate, all of you were put in danger because of me."

Grandfather tilted his head as he watched me. "So it is your fault that these men blackmailed your father when you were still a child? It is your fault that you could not stand not knowing who your father was?"

I swallowed the lump in my throat and said nothing. I was afraid to speak, not trusting the emotions just beneath the surface. Too many emotions had boiled over today, I didn't think I could survive anymore.

"You are not to blame for these things, Montana. You simply set into motion things that were started long before you had any control over them."

"I killed that man, Grandfather. That makes me no better than he was—a murderer." I finally said the one thing that weighed most heavily on my mind.

"His is not the first life you have taken."

I shook my head. "No, but he is the first one I wanted to. I still want to." My eyes locked on to the old man's in front of me. "If I could, I would make him live so I could do it all over again. That conflicts with everything I have ever been taught, but it doesn't make it any less true."

My grandfather considered this for a moment. "So you believe yourself to be an immoral man for these things you have done?"

"Yes, not just for the deeds, but for the thoughts."

My grandfather laughed at that. "If we were to be judged by our thoughts alone instead of our deeds, then hell would be quite the popular place. Let me ask you something, how do you live a moral and compassionate existence, when you are fully aware of the blood, the horror inherent in life, when you find darkness not only in your culture but within yourself? To be an adult is to grasp the irony in its unfolding and accept responsibility for a life lived in the midst of such a paradox. Life is one huge contradiction, Montana. There are simply no answers to some of life's most pressing questions. You just continue to live and try to guess right most of the time and in the end hope your life is a worthy expression of leaning as far into the light as you can get."

"I'm having a hard time seeing that light right about now," I told him.

He took a step toward me and drew me close to him in an unexpected embrace. I didn't know how badly I needed the simple human contact until he held me.

"And that is what family is for, to point you in the direction of that light when you can't find your way."

The simplicity of the statement brought me over the emotional precipice I had been teetering on. I wrapped my arms around this man, and I wept, for the past, for things I couldn't change, but I wept too, for the promise of the things yet to come. Things I might have some chance over yet. But most of all I simply wept until I emptied out all the ugliness I had felt boring a hole so deep within my soul.

CHAPTER 26

Tate drove my Jeep. That in itself should have told me just how far from centered I was. The other was the fact that despite everything, or perhaps because of it, five minutes into the drive I fell deeply, blissfully asleep. There were no dreams, nothing prophetic about it, just sleep.

I remembered nothing about the drive. Tate's gentle but insistent hand on my shoulder brought me back to reality. At first I resented the intrusion on the peace I had found, then on opening my eyes I realized where we were and sat up slowly, trying not to look as unfocused as I felt. The simple truth of the matter was that I could deny the demands of my body for only so long. I was tired, and I hurt in so many different ways.

"Hey." Tate's soft voice and understanding smile told me she saw exactly what I tried to conceal. "We're here," she confirmed for me.

I straightened in the seat, rubbed both hands over my face and tried to shake the exhaustion off. The neon sign on the side of the building declared we were indeed at Saint Vincent's Medical Center.

I looked across the seat at her. She canted her head and eyed me with intense scrutiny.

"What?" I asked after several long minutes under her gaze.

"You've looked better," she told me candidly.

"I've felt better too." Putting a hand on the door handle, I intended to open it when Tate stopped me.

"You sure you're up to this? I could go find Dad and bring him back here to give you a report." She nodded, apparently making up her mind. "Yeah, why don't you get some more sleep, I promise I'll get Dad for you."

I didn't even bother gracing the remark with a reply. I opened the door and looked around for a moment trying to orient myself. Tate had parked in the emergency room parking lot directly across from that department's entranceway. Without waiting for her, I walked in search of someone who could tell me where to find my brother.

Tate ran up beside me. "Well, it's not like I thought that was going to work, but I had to try." She entwined her arm through mine, pulling me in a different direction. "Not that way. Come on, I talked with Dad before I woke you up. He's waiting for us."

"Where?" I asked, letting her lead me.

"Second floor, surgical waiting room. You know, you really do look like shit, Montana."

I gave her my best sardonic smile. "Well, then that's a perfect match for how I feel. Can we go find out about my brother now?"

She smiled at me and pushed me in the right direction. David met us in the hallway just off the elevators.

"How is he?" I asked, ignoring his scrutiny. Obviously, Tate had shared more with him than just information on Dakota.

"Stable," David told me. "He's out of recovery and in a room. He still hasn't woken up from anesthesia yet."

"They were able to save his arm?" I knew what Walter had told me, but I needed to hear it again from David.

My father gave me a nod and a grin. "No problems. He needed a couple units of blood, but they repaired the artery. All he'll have to show for their efforts is a three-inch scar."

Immeasurable relief flooded through me, almost making me weak-kneed. I ran a hand through my hair and closed my eyes as I sighed. The relief, combined with my exhaustion, left my equilibrium off balance and I felt the room tilt a little under my feet. David caught me before I hit the ground and helped me slide down against the wall to sit on the floor.

Ignoring the concern I saw in his eyes, I concentrated on Dakota. "I want to see him," I said, looking back at my father.

"On one condition."

Narrowing my eyes in suspicion, I angled my face to better focus on him. "What?"

As my father stepped back, I saw a doctor in blue surgical scrubs standing just behind him.

"This is Doctor Salgado, Dakota's surgeon." My father introduced the man to me, and I got to my feet. The room spun a little, but I ignored it as I held my hand out to him.

Doctor Salgado took my hand and motioned to the waiting room a few feet away. "Why don't we sit?" he suggested.

"Why don't we go see my brother?" I offered instead.

The doctor exchanged a glance with my father and shook his head as he sighed.

"Because Walter Willowcreek is not only a respected colleague of mine but a trusted friend as well. When he calls and asks for my help with not one but two of his grandsons, I know he expects that request to be honored."

"You know my grandfather?" I asked.

"Very well. And as your father already told you, your brother is stable and still sleeping. He won't miss your charming presence for an hour or more at the very least."

"Why do I feel like a condition is coming up?"

"Because you're not stupid," Dr Salgado said with a smile. "Walter updated me on you, Montana Thomas. Now, if you want to see your brother, you have to allow me to look after you."

"I'm fine," I told him. I most definitely didn't like where this conversation was headed. I had just spent over a month flat on my back. The last thing I wanted was someone else poking at me.

"You just collapsed in my hallway. That does not make you fine in my book."

"Then get another book," I growled. "Look, I'm tired and worried about my brother, okay? That's all, just let me see Dakota." I was starting to get irritated and felt like I had been ambushed, but I let them lead me to a chair in the waiting room.

"Montana." My father squatted down next to the chair I sat in. "He's not asking you to take a room. All he wants is maybe thirty minutes of your time. You were not exactly in the most pristine of conditions lately, pal. We just want to make sure everything is working the way it should be. Then, I swear, I'll take you to Dakota."

I looked from my father to the doc and rubbed a hand over my face. I was too tired to fight them both. "This is blackmail, you realize that?"

"Whatever works." My father smiled.

"Thirty minutes?" I asked Doctor Salgado.

"More or less."

"Make it less," I told him.

I followed him down the hall to an exam room. After I'd stripped and put on the requisite blue paisley gown, Doctor Salgado thoroughly and professionally examined me. He drew some blood, cleaned and re-dressed my still healing arm. Then declaring I had a fever and was anemic, he told me I would benefit from a few days in the hospital. Holding up a hand and silencing me before I could object, he wrote me a prescription for a whopping dose of antibiotics.

"Take all of them," he told me.

I took the paper and gave him a nod of thanks.

"If you had ended up anyplace else but in Walter's hands, you'd be dead right now," he told me. "You owe that man your life."

"I owe him more than that," I said softly. Salgado didn't hear me, but he wasn't meant to. "I lived up to my end of the deal," I reminded him. "Can I see Dakota now?"

"Yeah, come on." He led me back to the waiting room where Tate and David sat.

"You go ahead," David said. "We'll wait here for you."

I nodded and followed Doctor Salgado down the hallway to where my brother waited.

A nurse who looked impossibly young hovered over him, a stethoscope pressed to his chest. An IV was secured to his arm and oxygen tubing curled in his nose. His face was the color of porcelain, the black hair and lashes standing out in stark relief. His left arm was bandaged from wrist to shoulder. Hell of a lot of bandages for a three-inch scar.

The nurse smiled at me and spoke in a whisper. "He's awake. Just sleepy yet. Let me know if you have any questions or need anything." With a flick of her blond ponytail she left to speak with Doctor Salgado standing just outside the room looking over Dakota's chart.

I ignored them, stepped over to the bed and pulled up a chair. He didn't look awake. I sat there afraid to touch him, so I just watched his chest rise and fall gently with the rhythm of his breathing. The slow, quiet rhythm made me sleepy, and I found my eyes sliding closed.

"You know, I think there's a rule only one of us can get hurt at a time."

My eyes snapped open at the soft words. I couldn't quite keep the smile from my face as Dakota's eyes met mine.

"Then you should have realized it wasn't your turn yet."

"My timing was a little off. Forgive me."

"Consider yourself forgiven." I scooted forward in the chair, reaching for his hand. "How you doing, man?"

"Tired, but in one piece. How about you? What was the endgame, Montana? I don't remember."

"Good guys won for a change."

"We got them?" he asked.

"Decimated and cremated." I grinned.

"Cremated? Really? Wow, that seems a little, I don't know, barbaric." He gave me a quiet laugh. "I guess we're not supposed to know anything about what happened, huh?"

"No one has asked me any questions, I haven't seen one cop. Apparently Grandpa Walt has some pretty impressive connections."

"So, what? We're going on the 'don't ask, don't tell' principle?"

I had no idea what Dakota knew about what happened. Personally, I wanted to leave it that way. I knew Walter was moving the camp and would destroy any evidence of the battle that had ensued there. If Mike and his men went missing, it would turn into another unsolved mystery, landing in a cold-case file in the basement of some police department. As far as I was concerned, justice had been served.

"Works for me," I said.

"You okay?" he asked me.

"I'm not the one in the hospital," I reminded him.

"Looks like you should be."

Shaking my head in frustration, I stood and hovered over him. "Yeah, maybe, but I'm the one leaving now. You know, I am having a very clear memory of you stripping me naked when I was in a compromised position." Lifting the covers and peeking underneath I saw he was dressed only in a thin hospital gown. "Close enough," I said and gave him a wicked grin.

"Go away, Montana," Dakota said, snatching the covers back with his good arm.

"Oh, yeah, not a problem. I'll leave, but you know who came with me?"

Dakota looked at me in confusion.

"Must be the drugs," I told him. "You're usually much quicker than this. Tate is waiting just outside. I hear you are in desperate need of a bath. I'll go get her, I think they saved all the good parts for her."

A look of realization spread across his face. "No freaking way, Montana!"

I ducked as he threw the only thing he could reach, an empty plastic urinal.

"Payback's a bitch, man." I laughed as I walked out the door to go get Tate and our father. I realized it had been a very long time since I had anything at all to laugh about. It felt good.

* * * *

Three days later Dakota was discharged with strict instructions for return appointments and physical therapy. They'd had to replace over half his entire body's volume of blood, but he looked good. His cheeks had a healthy glow to them and he was driving the medical staff insane, a very good indicator to me as to how well he was really feeling. If he could bitch because his coffee wasn't hot enough he was ready to leave.

After three days of antibiotics, I was feeling a lot more like myself too. The problem was, I had no idea where to go or what to do. It had been exactly eight weeks since my mother died and I had heard the name Jacob Willowcreek for the first time.

How long does it take to change a life forever? For me, the answer was a short eight weeks. I had lost a mother, nearly lost my life and my brother, but I had also gained a father, a sister, two grandfathers, my Santee and an entire culture that had been denied to me from almost the moment of my birth. All because of a secret kept protecting my brother and myself from what? My father and his past? Despite everything I had been through in the last few weeks, it just didn't reconcile with me.

David had secured two adjoining rooms at a nearby motel. Dakota waited for me at the hospital while I packed up my few meager belongings and prepared to leave. I turned with the last load in my arms and found my father in the open doorway. In the harsh light of the early morning, he looked older than I remembered. Deep lines etched around his eyes and mouth, he looked, I imagined, how I would in a decade or two.

"You're leaving." It wasn't a question, but a simple statement of fact.

I nodded and raised my brows. "Yeah, adventure completed." I tried to make light of what we had so recently been through.

"Where you headed?" he asked me.

"Back to Caliente, I guess, to start. I need to get Dakota back in school." I hiked my shoulders in acceptance. "It's home," I said simply.

"It's not your only home, not anymore. You do know that, don't you?"

"Do I?" I knew this man standing before me was my father. I knew that without a doubt, but I was having a little difficulty accepting him as anything more than that just yet.

David leaned against the doorway and crossed his arms over his chest as he watched me. "Look, Montana, I'm not asking for you to start sending me Father's Day cards or anything."

"What exactly are you asking then, David?"

"A chance, maybe?"

I had to laugh at that. "You kind of missed the boat on the father thing. I don't need a father. I don't need you, not anymore. You weren't there when I did, you can't expect to make up for that now." I knew how the words sounded, harsh and unforgiving. I didn't really care. I may have forgiven him for leaving us, I might even have understood on some level, but in no way did that mean I had to let the man into my life. I guess if I was completely honest with myself, I wanted to hurt him and the only weapon I had at my disposal was words.

If my words hit home, I never knew, his face remained completely neutral. He pushed off the wall, reached inside his pocket and withdrew a folded piece of paper. He stepped just far enough inside the room to lay it on the bedside table as if he expected me to react exactly as I did.

"My cellphone number and email address, my father's and Tate's too," he explained. "I understand if you don't want anything more to do with me, but don't make them suffer for something I did, something they had no control over. My mother expects you to visit."

I looked at the paper, but didn't touch it—not yet. "Where are you headed?" I asked him.

He hitched his shoulders as he walked back out the door. "Ekalaka, it's home," he said. "I'll rebuild. You know where to find me, if you want to."

He turned his back on me and walked two, maybe three steps before turning back to face me.

"I'm sorry, Montana." He opened his mouth to say more and shook his head, I think at the futility of words. "I'm sorry," he repeated.

I watched him walk away, this man I had spent a lifetime trying to find. That old adage came to mind: *be careful what you wish for, you just might get it.*

David never looked back. He got in the Range Rover and backed it out of the parking lot. As he turned the vehicle around, I met Tate's eyes in the passenger seat. She put her hand on the window and spread her fingers as if she were trying to reach through the glass to me. I raised my hand, fingers spread in a silent goodbye to her. I followed her eyes as long as I could and stayed liked that, hand raised for some time even after the Rover was long out of sight.

I don't remember ever feeling so alone as I did in those few moments in that motel parking lot. Walking back inside the room, I took one last look around and then spied the numbers David had left for me. My initial instinct was to rip the paper up and throw the pieces to the wind. In fact I crumpled the sheet in my hand preparing to do just that, but something stopped me. Smoothing the wrinkles out, I opened the folded piece of paper. As promised, my father's contact numbers were listed as were Tate's and Walter's. At the bottom in a sprawling legible handwriting I assumed was David's was a short quote:

You often meet fate on the road you seek to avoid it.

I must have stood there in the open doorway of that motel room and read that sentence a hundred times. I probably would have read it a hundred more if the housekeeper hadn't knocked softly on the doorframe to get my attention.

"You go now?" she asked in heavily accented English.

I looked up at her a little startled, folded the paper and put it in my back pocket. I gave her a smile and the key. "Oh, yeah, just have to pay the bill and I'm out of here."

"No, no pay. Meester Dave, he say he pay, you all good." She smiled at me. "You go now?"

"Yeah, I go now."

I pulled open the door to the Jeep and just sat there in the driver's seat for a minute. The sun had heated the inside of the vehicle, and I laid my head back and enjoyed the warmth seeping through to my bones.

Deciding I had wasted enough time, I put the key in the ignition and pushed the clutch in. I moved my hand to the gear stick when I felt something beneath my fingers.

I glanced down at the stick and saw something wrapped around it. My heart found its way to my throat as I recognized what I was looking at. Unwinding the leather cord, I held up the coyote fetish necklace I had left in Ekalaka just before my whole world turned upside down.

My father had found it. He had found it and he had kept it for me. I closed my fist around the small piece of turquoise that was so much more than a hunk of stone, and squeezed my eyes closed, trying to will the past to change. When that predictably failed, I took a deep breath and put the necklace around my neck. It felt heavier than I remembered, it also felt comforting. I placed the fetish beneath my shirt and placed my hand over it. I could feel the beat of my heart beneath my hand, the warmth of my flesh contrasting with the chill of the rock on my skin. In a few minutes, I knew it would warm to my body temperature, in effect becoming part of me once more. Just like everything that had happened to me had become a part of me. Just like David Willows had become a part of me, had in fact always been a part of me. It was an irrefutable fact that I couldn't ignore and one I didn't want to confront just yet.

I put the Jeep in gear and headed out of the parking lot to pick up my brother and take us both home. It was a trip, I realized, that was long overdue.

Epilogue

Dusk comes early to the desert. The darkness didn't concern me, it never did. I always felt at home here in the dark. I always felt as if I were one with the creatures of the night, the ones that huddle in dark corners to sleep while the sun holds court and bakes the earth. The ones that come to life only after the sun lays her head down behind the hills to rest and lets her brother, the moon, spread his cool light across the land.

The way back to my desert campsite was ingrained in my memory. I found my tent just as I had left it the day Cal had taken me to say goodbye to my mother. Deer mice had shredded my sleeping bag, using the down stuffing as nesting material. Larger animals had found my meager food supplies and eaten or destroyed anything worth having. I had expected as much and brought replacements for everything I knew would no longer be usable after so much time left to the night and her creatures.

It took me a good hour to set everything right and make my little camp habitable again. By that time, the moon had gone from a muted orange ball just above the buttes to a brilliant, cool ivory light giving life to the night. Dragging my sleeping bag out of the tent, I brought it into the open and lay down on it looking up at the stars. The sky was a living thing. Every light in the cosmos was shining there for my viewing pleasure. The scent of yucca and sage, night blooming jasmine and moonflowers came to me on the slight breeze. It also carried with it the scent of the desert itself. Life existed here despite all odds against it. Maybe that was the attraction, my lifelong fascination with this place.

I felt more at peace here than I had in a long time. Dakota had mended quickly and gone back to finish school at the beginning of the last semester. I kept in touch with him a lot more closely than I had in the past. I kept my father's number close at hand, I still hadn't used it, but it wasn't something I considered an impossibility either.

My job in Denver no longer appealed to me. I gave the law firm I had worked for notice. I had an idea what I wanted to do with my life, but for now all I really wanted was to lie in the quiet darkness of the desert night and just *be.*

I felt myself drifting off, lulled to sleep by the sounds and rhythms of the night, when a disturbance, a sound that I hadn't heard before caused me to open my eyes. Moving slowly, not knowing what had made the sound that woke me, I pushed up to one elbow and found myself staring into the yellow, almost hypnotic eyes of a coyote no more than five feet away from me.

I froze and just stared back. It was unusual to see a lone coyote, they are pack animals and seldom travel alone. Maybe this one had been used to scavenging at my abandoned campsite and I had surprised it by being here. But if that were the case, it should have just run away when it noticed me.

It didn't. In fact it seemed quite fascinated by me. It paced in front of me for a while, then apparently satisfied I wasn't about to harm it, it sat down on its haunches, cocked its head and looked directly at me. It was thin, but not to the point of starvation. Its coarse gray coat was flecked with tan, brown and black. Long, lanky and lean, it defied everything by simply staying there.

"What do you want?" I asked the creature.

The coyote's ears flicked forward at the sound of my voice, but it never moved. Sitting up, I sat cross-legged and we continued our very strange staring contest. All the stories my mother had ever told me while sitting with her in the cool of the Nevada desert came to mind.

"*Do you hear them, Montana?*"

"I hear them, Mama," I whispered, looking at the coyote sitting in front of me.

"*What are they saying?*"

"That my father loves us."

"*Listen to the coyotes, Montana. They need someone to hear their songs.*"

My mother's last words to me.

Without warning the coyote sprang to its feet, threw its head back to the full moon above it and howled. It was a lonely, mournful sound, almost like crying. When it was finished it lowered its head and cocked it, listening. I listened too. I heard it then, the answering howl my coyote had been waiting for, then another and another. And all the while my coyote simply stood and stared at me as if it were waiting for something.

I was surrounded by the songs of the coyote and I think I got it. I thought I might have finally understood what my mother was trying to tell me. It wasn't a literal lesson she so desperately tried to get across to her very analytical child, but a figurative one.

Coyotes may appear lonely, but they are always in touch with their pack. They crave what we all do in the end. Simple contact with their own kind, their family. My mother was trying to give me permission to find my father, to find him and love him.

She knew I craved isolation, but she also knew that being alone and being lonely were two completely different things. It took me thirty years to learn that lesson.

You often meet fate on the road you seek to avoid it.

My father's word echoed back to me and suddenly mirrored what I felt my mother had tried to teach me as a child.

The coyote answered its brothers with one long mournful wail, then gave me a soulful last look through yellow-hazed eyes—I swear the thing looked human just for a moment—before loping off to find its pack and the evening meal.

I listened to the coyotes sing for another hour or more, their song so much more beautiful to my ears than in years gone by.

"I hear them, Mama," I said, looking up to the stars above me. "I hear the coyote's song."

Then on a whim and totally unaware of the time, I took a dog-eared piece of paper out of my wallet and pulled my cellphone out of my backpack and turned it on. Two bars, I wasn't sure if the signal would be strong enough, but I was committed to trying.

I punched the numbers into the luminous panel and waited for the connection to go through. My palms grew damp as the line started ringing.

On the sixth ring I pulled the phone away from my ear intending to disconnect when a sleep-filled voice answered on the other end.

I placed the phone back to my ear and took a deep, steadying breath.

"Dad, it's Montana. I was hoping maybe we could talk."

In the cool of the desert night, the coyotes sang.

About Ann Simko

When I first wrote *Fallen* in 2005, Montana was a minor character. He didn't even warrant a full chapter. Then I had the raw manuscript read by a critique group and everyone wanted more of the man. So I rewrote *Fallen* and the Montana you now know was born (and in case you're wondering—he is not my favorite. That honor goes to Dakota.)

The Coyote's Song was my way of getting to know Montana a little better. I wanted to understand the things that drove him; I wanted to hear the noise behind his silence. I hope you like the Montana I discovered, I know I do. In fact, I hope you want to read more about him because the next book I hope to have out soon has Montana in the spotlight once more. Thank you for visiting my world for a little while—I hope you enjoyed your stay.

Ann's Website:

http://www.annsimko.com/

Reader eMail:

absimko@ptd.net

author@swvaughn.com

About the Coyote Moon Series

Book 1: *Fallen*

Available in ebook from Lyrical Press

Book 2: *Through the Glass*

Available in ebook from Lyrical Press

Book 3: *The Coyote's Song*

Available in ebook from Lyrical Press

Breinigsville, PA USA
25 October 2010
248061BV00001B/7/P